INFINITE GESTURES

Thank you –
Dick

Stories by

RICHARD V. BARRY

Winterlight Books

Shelbyville, KY USA

Infinite Gestures
by Richard V. Barry

First Printing – November 2012
ISBN: 978-1-60047-803-1

Printed in the U.S.A.

0   1   2   3   4   5   6   7

BOOKS BY RICHARD V. BARRY

Short Stories

CROSSCURRENTS: Stories of People in Conflict

PERSONAL WARS

Novels

AN INCONVENIENT DEATH

QUALITIES OF MERCY

IN EVIL'S VORTEX

TO

PROFESSORS SIMON AND SUNNY TREFFMAN,
who believed in second chances.

Table of Contents

Roots Planted Deep

George Washington Clark surveyed the destruction all around him and immediately thought of passages from The Bible where God destroyed cities. He started quoting long passages to himself as he sifted through the rubble of his house. That is, he *thought* he was quoting passages to himself; he could never be sure. Lately, when he thought he was speaking in his mind, some one would draw attention to hearing him talking aloud. That would confuse and embarrass him into complete silence.

The Bible had been his constant companion for all his eighty-seven years. The first words he could recall hearing his mother say were from the Old Testament. As a young boy, she had told him that he came from a long line of people with the gift of preaching and soothing the hurts of others, even when they were still slaves. As he grew into manhood, he hoped that he, too, had been given the gift, but it never came. Still, he studied his Bible steadfastly throughout his long life. He had buried two wives and four children and never lost faith in the Lord. Now he needed that faith more than ever.

"Come away, Daddy. Come away," he heard the coaxing voice of his only living child, his daughter Viola, as she gently tugged at his sleeve. He shrugged her off. He squinted in the bright sun as he kicked at the rubble.

"I got to find the pictures," he said in a defiant tone. "That's all I want: the pictures."

Viola recognized the steely glint in her father's voice but she still held him by his sleeve, fearful that with his poor eyesight he would stumble over the mounds of debris and hurt himself. He had broken an arm a few years back and it had taken a long time to heal. She looked disconsolately at the moonscape of rubble that had been the house she grew up in and started to cry. Her father ignored her, shuffling forward unsteadily, his watery eyes, glazed with cataracts, fixed on the few feet in front of him.

The hurricane that swept across this section of the Florida panhandle had baffled all the experts with its sudden, unexpected turn in trajectory just before approaching land and, now officially designated as a Category Two, was strong enough to damage buildings not up to code. His house had been the oldest one in the area and, along with one other on the long block, had collapsed. Miraculously, all other houses had suffered only minor damage.

As a child, Viola had always felt safe and secure in this house and now she realized how flimsy it must have been. It had been built by her father's father and added to by her father. Built on love and determination, she thought, if not a lot of real knowledge of house building. The house was in a poor black area that was largely ignored by the city fathers; codes were not systematically enforced and few services tendered.

As soon as the hurricane had moved on, Viola had driven the hundred and fifty miles north to check on her father, never expecting to find his home in total ruin. Her mind was now racing as she tried to formulate a plan for her father's future. For years she had invited—urged—him to move in with her. She had a small rented house which, with three of her six children and two grandchildren all living with her—and, now that she was divorced, an occasional boyfriend—was bursting at the seams. He had adamantly refused.

"This is where I be born and this is where I wants to die," he'd say repeatedly, and, seeing the fierce resolve in his eyes, she usually dropped the subject.

Now his house was gone. He had no home and she had to do something, and quick. But he could be so difficult. She thought, with relief, that at least he had sense enough to take shelter in the root cellar when the house started to crumble around him. His neighbors got him out as soon as the storm had passed and had taken him in until she got there. Now she had to find a permanent solution.

He got a small social security check each month and perhaps he could rent a small apartment in her town so she could look after him without overcrowding her already overcrowded house. That might be the answer. Give him the independence he still demanded but still keep an eye on him.

He bent down and pushed a broken kitchen chair aside and then an upended side table.

"Here it is!" he cried excitedly, slowly straightening his body and clutching a dusty, ragged photograph album in his arms. "The pictures!" For the first time since her arrival, he smiled. She smiled, too. How often, as a small child, she had sat at his side, gazing at the sepia-toned pictures as he told her stories of her grandparents who were all dead by the time she, as the last child of his second wife, had arrived. There was even a small, badly faded picture of her great grandmother who had been born a slave—a concept she could not grasp until she was much older. For each picture he told her of struggles and difficulties, but he also related funny stories about them, and she sensed, even as a small child, his great, abiding pride in them.

She especially liked looking at the pictures of her mother who had died of cancer when she was only two years old. She never tired of hearing his stories about her mother: how he met her, how pretty she was, how happy they had been before her diagnosis, long illness and sorrowful death.

He brushed the dirt and dust from the album cover with his sleeve, still smiling.

"Now can we go, Daddy?" she asked, taking him by the elbow. She felt his body stiffen.

"Go where?" he asked, his smile fading into a look of confusion.

"To my house," she said with forced cheerfulness. "I'll make you a nice dinner, and all the kids will be happy to see you."

He took a step backwards, stumbling over some wood but regaining his balance, and looked sternly at his daughter.

"That's too far. I can't go there," he said as his eyes now darted around the remnants of his home.

"Daddy, honey," she said as though talking to a little child, "where else can we go?"

He didn't answer and she could see his confusion growing as he looked wildly about him. Then, as if he had found an answer, he said in a decisive voice, "I want to stay here!"

"Here?" she asked. Now she was confused.

"Here!" he repeated, even more firmly.

"But you can't stay here, Daddy," she said patiently. "Your home is gone!" She made a sweeping gesture with her arm and then reached to take hold again of his elbow, but he shrugged her off. She saw the tears welling in his eyes.

"This where I be born and this where I'll die," he said, his voice cracking.

"Daddy, be reasonable," she protested. "You don't even have a place to sleep."

A frantic look flashed across his face as he searched for a solution to the latest challenge his daughter had given him. Finally his white eyebrows lifted and his eyes widened. "I can stay with Old Peter," he said, shifting his gaze toward the small, ragged house, standing intact, just beyond the tangled rubble.

She followed his gaze and thought of Old Peter—she called him Uncle Peter when she was little—who was several years older than her father and living alone.

"He told me this morning that I could stay with him," he said jubilantly.

Viola weighed this news with some skepticism at first, followed by a growing sense of relief. She knew that Peter had children living in town who checked up on him, so if anything happened to her father, they'd let her know. The two families had been neighbors for over fifty years and she thought how nice it would be for the two old men to share a home and be company for each other. She could drive up every month or so to see him, but, this way, she wouldn't have to worry about finding him a place in her town and getting him settled in.

She remembered how his few visits to her home had not gone well. Her grandkids—his great grandkids—got on his nerves and she knew he would never approve of her having a boyfriend living in the house. And to uproot him at this age didn't seem fair. Her face brightened as she concluded that moving in with Peter might be a practical solution. Her thoughts were interrupted by her father's voice, stronger now.

"I'll rebuild it," was what she thought she heard him say, but that was so preposterous, she couldn't be sure.

"What, Daddy?" she asked.

"I'm gonna rebuild it," he said, and his jaw locked in place, as she had seen so many times when he had made a decision and persuasion was useless. Still, she was shocked.

"But, Daddy, honey, you don't have the money to rebuild," she said in a little-girl voice that she hoped would gently coax him back to reality.

His jaw muscles twitched as he surveyed the wreckage again. "I'll rebuild it myself," he said firmly.

It was hopeless to argue. This was an old man's fantasy and why should she try to shake him awake?

"I'll start tomorrow," he announced, a smile deepening the heavy creases around his mouth. "Old Peter will help me."

She recalled that Peter suffered from severe arthritis and a heart condition, but all she said was "Sure, Daddy. Okay."

He let her take his elbow now and lead him, with the photograph album clutched tightly in her arms, across the rubble to Peter's house.

* * * *

The next morning it was barely light when George Washington Clark appeared among the ruins of his house and began to work. Neighbors, peaking out of their windows to check on the weather, were astonished to see the frail old man, moving slowly and deliberately, selecting small pieces of debris and, with obvious effort, carrying them to the curb in a laborious shuffle.

Some neighbors went off to work, as normal life resumed in the community, waving at the funny old man so intent in his labors that he didn't wave back. He had been a fixture on the block for as long as anyone could remember and the younger men called him Pops. When they came home from work, he was still there and a small pile was now visible at the curb.

Each day of that week, from early morning to just before dusk, there he was, ceaselessly carrying small armloads of his shattered home to the curb, breathing heavily but with a fixed stare. Some days, neighbors would see Old Peter, bent over his cane, standing on the sidelines, speaking occasionally but mostly watching in silence.

When the weekend came, some of the younger men wandered over to visit Pops, assuming he was sifting the wreckage looking for valued possessions. Never stopping his work, Pops would answer their casual questions, and it was only then that they realized his intention to rebuild. A few laughed out loud, while others humored the old man and admired his foolhardy grit.

Without any invitation and not asking for permission, one man, a construction worker, moved into the rubble and started carrying larger pieces to the curb. Another man came and joined him; then another. Disregarding the minor repairs needed to their own homes, by early Saturday afternoon, at least a half-dozen men, mostly young but some clearly middle-age and one man in his seventies, had haphazardly formed a crew of workers, and the pile at the curb by the end of the day had reached an impressive height.

Pops never said anything but worked alongside of them until their wives were calling them to super and still he continued working until the sky turned dark. He seemed to grow frailer and smaller with each day but he never stopped.

On Sunday afternoon, instead of lounging at home, watching sports programs, most of the men reappeared, joined now by new volunteers, including a few women who were good at spying small objects among the rubble. Most people took note of the smile on Pops' face.

All of the men were laborers who worked hard during the week and who viewed the weekend as a time for rest and relaxation. But this spontaneous joining together with neighbors to help an old man who seemed so valiantly dedicated, so extravagantly and ridiculously committed to his singular goal of rebuilding his home and replanting his roots, inspired them to join his cause. Come Sunday night, after two days of hard work for more hours than their regular jobs demanded, they felt more refreshed, more replenished, more content than they could remember.

On Monday, the pile at the curb had been carted away. Returning from work, the men on the block knew that Pops was still at it. Like a virus, a new spirit infected the neighborhood, as word spread to other blocks about the crazy old man who had a dream. The owners of the house at the other end of the curvilinear block that had been destroyed by the hurricane had abandoned it and moved away. Not Pops. His relentless desire to stay where he had always been was taken as a validation of his neighbors and his community.

The next weekend more men from adjacent blocks showed up and quietly joined in the work, exchanging nods and smiles with men they hadn't known before but with whom they now felt an instant bond. Several wives made sandwiches and brought them, along with lemonade and homemade cookies, to the work site so the work could continue uninterrupted. By the second Sunday the pile at the curb was huge and someone had the foresight to call the town and advise them to send an extra truck.

One neighbor who worked as a construction manager had organized a small crew to salvage those materials that could be used for rebuilding, and that separate pile lay in the rear of the property. As the men surveyed it, they realized that they had joined in the enterprise to clear the land on impulsive desires to help, but had given no thought to the project envisioned by Pops to rebuild his house. This complicated reality now set in, and many questions, without easy answers, arose like dark clouds on the horizon. But looking at Pops and his cloudless determination, they thought, hell, there must be a way. Day after day they saw this frail old man, his jaw set, his blurry eyes staring straight ahead, endlessly working at his slow-but-steady pace and they were inspired. Hope and optimism were carrying them along, but practical matters had to be addressed. By now, though, every man was invested in Pops' dream.

The damaged rocking chair that had always been on Pops' narrow front porch had been retrieved from the rubble and repaired by a neighbor who was a carpenter. Just before nightfall, neighbors could glimpse Pops sitting in the rocking chair, placed exactly where his front porch had been, rocking away contentedly. Everyone who saw him smiled, sharing in his joy, proud of their communal effort.

* * * *

Later that same night, neighbors heard Old Peter calling for help. A few men in the nearby houses rushed across the street. They found Old Peter standing next to the rocking chair and Pops was still sitting in it, but slumped over. A brief check of his pulse told the story: Pops was dead.

Viola was called and arrived the next day to claim her father's body. She arranged for a one-day wake at the local funeral home. From early morning to late evening, people she had never met streamed in, and what was more amazing, they seemed to be genuinely saddened by her father's passing. From all their comments, she pieced together the recent transformation in the neighborhood that her father had brought about with his tenacious dream.

"He was a brave old man," said one neighbor, while another said, "He inspired us all." And on and on and on. By the end of the exhausting day, Viola's head was filled with the echoes of warm comments, many from strangers. But the one she remembered most was Old Peter's: "He died happy, knowing he could stay where his roots be."

Her father was not the kind of man to talk about death, and she now recalled that he had never expressed any desires to her about disposal of his body. His parents were buried in one local cemetery, but his two wives and four dead children, her siblings, were buried in another cemetery. Then another idea emerged. She weighed alternatives and, with Old Peter's observation foremost in her mind, decided what she would do. Now she had to tell the funeral director about her plans for her father.

The following night was cloudless and lit by a half moon. Viola drove her car to her father's property and stood at the curb. All that remained of the house she had grown up in were some concrete blocks that outlined the original foundation and the pile of salvaged boards and beams. This was a community of laborers who rose early and went to bed early, and the lights in the neighboring homes were out. Somewhere down the block she heard a dog bark, then stop. Silence enveloped her, and in her imagination the shadows cast by the moonlight against the surrounding houses and the barren trees, stripped by the hurricane, gave the land a spectral gloom. She could almost hear the voices of her grandparents, her mother and father, her brothers and sisters. She opened the urn that contained her father's ashes and, walking slowly from front to back, swung the urn from side to side, letting the tan powder drift casually across the ground.

When she reached the rear of the property, she turned and, seeing an opalescent glow suffusing the cratered land, quietly spoke her personal eulogy.

"Rest in peace, Daddy. You're home."

The Woman Who Thought She Could Dance

When my brother Timothy brought his new wife, Clare, back east to meet the family at our annual summer clan gathering, we were all shocked.   Second wives of successful middle-age men are supposed to be eye candy, right?   She should be much younger and not too sophisticated so she can look in endless admiration at her wiser, more mature spouse. She should have a great shape, taut muscles, long legs and unflagging energy in the sack. Well, that's how I pictured my second wife if I had the guts to divorce Joanne and was willing to beggar my lifestyle after she took me to the cleaners. Only joking!

Anyway, when Timothy arrived with Clare, my two other brothers and their snooty wives had the same reaction as Joanne and I did. So many jaws dropped in shock that you'd think we were witnessing the Second Coming. Even from fifty feet away, as Timothy and

Clare crossed the wide lawn of my bother Peter's Southampton beach house, I could see that Clare was not my image of wife number two. Hell, she wasn't anyone's image of a second wife unless you were eighty, senile and desperate.

For starters, she looked at least five years older than Timothy, which would have placed her in the mid-fifties range. If you were kind, you might describe her figure as ample or robust or like a Rubens' painting. But it was a safe bet that neither Joanne nor my two other sisters-in-law would use any descriptors but fat or gross, since these women lived on a diet of watercress, coffee, yogurt and dried fruit, proud of their swizzle-stick silhouettes and size two dresses.

Clare was wearing a lime green pant suit and a lot of clanking silver jewelry.

"My god, she looks like a Christmas tree," whispered Roberta, Peter's wife, as we all stood on the front terrace to greet our oldest brother and his new wife.

"Stephanie must be turning over in her grave," snickered Constance, my other sister-in-law, referring to Timothy's first wife of seventeen years who had literally starved herself to death but who, even at eighty-four pounds, was known as a fashion plate.

I could see that the knives were out and this newest addition to our family was prime meat for slicing, dicing and carving.

Clare was waving extravagantly to us as she stumbled across the grass in stiletto heels, her chubby cheeks ballooning in a huge smile, her shoulder-length dyed blond hair tossed by the ocean breezes and swirling about her head like a lemon Slurpee. *The lamb being led to the slaughter*, I thought. *She doesn't realize what a nest of vipers she's approaching.*

When I say that this occasion was the annual gathering of our clan, I don't mean to imply that we were a gathering of extended family members: cousins and aunts and uncles and in-laws and such. We were much more exclusive. After Timothy, the oldest, there was my brother Peter, our host, and his wife, Roberta. Joseph was the third oldest and Constance was his wife. Joanne and I brought up the rear.

Timothy had followed his bliss and struck out for California after graduating from college—actually, he was following his first wife, Stephanie, whom he had met in college and who had returned to her family in Los Angeles Timothy was now the literary agent for several very successful writers, As for the rest of us, my brothers Peter and Joseph and I—my name is Mark, by the way— were partners in the Monroe Brothers law firm, started by our father and uncle, located in Manhattan and specializing in tax law.

As our law firm continued to grow and prosper, we all acquired wives who eagerly aspired with us to upward mobility. All three wives were fiercely competitive and spent as little time as possible in one another's company. But this weekend-long summer gathering at Peter's impressive ocean-front spread was an established tradition that the wives reluctantly went along with. All our kids were away at exclusive summer camps each year—their mothers' finding it much too stressful to cope with them when they were out of school—so they were never part of this reunion. Any surviving parents were safely tucked away in nursing homes or ensconced in Florida condos.

My wife used to say that this weekend was like joining King Lear's two daughters, Goneril and Regan, for some summer fun, but I knew from long experience that Joanne was no Cordelia and could be as waspish as Roberta and Constance. Now all three women seemed suddenly united and dipped in vitriol, ready to pounce on the large, gaudy, ebullient lady approaching us, waving her arms exuberantly and shouting "Hello. Hello. Hello!"

"This is better than vaudeville," Roberta said through the clenched-teeth smile she bestowed on anyone she considered her inferior, as Timothy and Clare, huffing and puffing as though she had just scaled Mount Everest, finally reached the stone terrace fronting Peter's home. Like a military phalanx, we all marched forward to greet them.

"Welcome!" Peter said in his robust baritone, as Joseph and I exchanged awkward shoulder rubbings and back slaps with Timothy.

The three wives gave Clare their frostiest smiles, like Greek goddesses deigning to appear before a mortal, eyebrows arched disdainfully, arms extended at rigid right angles from their bodies. But Clare wasn't playing her part. Ignoring the distance-defending arm extensions, she grabbed each woman in turn and enveloped her in a bear hug as well as a big sloppy kiss on the cheek, thereby smudging makeup that had been meticulously applied to create that fresh, dewy girls-on-the-beach illusion.

Stunned into silence by such effrontery, the three wives stood motionless, frozen smiles turning into dour grimaces, as Clare overwhelmed them with both her physical aggression and her non-stop chattering.

"I'm so happy to meet you all. Timmy hasn't told me much about ya, but that's okay 'cause I can get to know ya myself. What a beautiful place this is! So big! And that ocean right at your doorstep! That was quite a trek we had from the car. I'm tuckered out. Now first off, let me be sure I get all your names straight." She pointed a hand, adorned with multi-colored nails and several silver rings, at each wife. "Let's see now, it's Joanne, Roberta and Constance, right? Lovely names! Easy to remember, but harder to know what name goes with who. But I'm a fast learner. I had to learn all my customers' names. It helped my business."

The left eyebrow on all three wives lifted into a pronounced arch as a mental communication suggested Clare might be referring to the world's oldest profession.

Now Clare turned her attention to the men. "And these are all my handsome brother-in-laws.," she shouted. (She actually said brother-in-laws.) She repeated her effusive greeting by flinging her arms around each of us and delivering another loud cheek smooch. A heavy perfume assaulted my nostrils as her large breasts imprinted on my shirt.

I'm proud to say that we brothers responded a little more enthusiastically to Clare's overtures, returning her hugs with some gentle pats, while the wives looked on in amazement. They could not have been more discombobulated, more stunned if that odious Democrat, Bill Clinton, has suddenly appeared before them, naked, shaking his wanky at them. These women who prided themselves on their sophistication, their *sang-froid* and their religious dedication to never being *non-plused*, were now reduced to blank-eyed ice sculptures by this blathering spectacle before them.

Our brother Timothy had always been on the quiet side which, I reflected, was a good thing since Clare was talking faster than an auctioneer in the final throes of a heated bidding war, with everyone surrounding her subdued into stunned silence. Score one for Clare, I thought jubilantly.

"I have to tinkle," Clare announced with not a trace of self-consciousness, but I saw Joanne wince. We all headed into the house.

"I'll show you to your room," Roberta said frostily.

"Great!" exclaimed Clare. "I'd like to get out of these traveling duds and into somethin' more comfortable."

"Pajamas?" Joanne asked archly as Clare followed Roberta up the stairs. Clare erupted in a loud guffaw. "No, honey, just somethin' cooler."

Timothy was obediently following Clare with a suitcase in each hand.

"Why don't we meet in the library in a half-hour for drinks," Peter said, glancing at his watch.

From the top of the stairs, Clare called down, "But I'd like to take a swim first. All that beautiful water is callin' to me."

"Then we'll have drinks by the pool," Peter said.

"I don't mean the pool," Clare responded. "I mean the ocean."

We all stood at the bottom of the stairs in another grip of stunned silence. If Clare had said she wanted to go bungee jumping off the George Washington Bridge, we could not have been more surprised.

`The ocean, with its rolling waves and their noisy landings on white sandy beaches, was a languorously beautiful prop that supplied atmosphere and cachet to the estates perched on its borders. The owners of these estates and their guests might stroll along the shore, taking in the salt air and ocean rhythms, but except for their teenage children, no one ever set a toe in the dipping phosphorescent waves. Roberta and Peter did laps in their sixty-foot, salt-water pool for exercise, but Constance and Joanne rigorously protected their hair and skin from any water that was not coming from a faucet or, preferably, a bottle.

"I don't know about the rest of you, but I need a drink," my brother Joseph said, after Clare and Timothy had disappeared into their appointed guest room, and we all trooped through the house to the bar on the rear terrace. Peter mixed a batch of Absolut martinis as we sat around the curved mahogany bar and eyed one another.

"Where did he ever find her?" was Joseph's first remark after taking a generous swig of his drink and shaking his head in disbelief.

"He met her at some party in L. A.," Peter said. "She's a hairdresser, I think he said. Comes from Arkansas or Iowa—some place foreign."

We all chuckled.

"If poor Stephanie could see what's replaced her, she'd never believe it," Joanne said. "She'd rise right up out of her grave and start eating corn dogs and chocolate tarts."

"Whatever possessed Timothy?" Constance asked.

"Senility seems to have struck him at an early age," Joseph said. "And what about her calling him Timmy? No one's ever dared call him that."

"Senility is the only logical explanation," Joanne said. "Did you see how he stood there, just grinning at her from ear to ear, like she was Princess Di?"

"He seems totally smitten," I offered.

"Maybe she's great in the sack. Those thunder thighs!" Peter quipped.

I caught Constance and Joanne exchanging brief, awkward glances. Sexual athletics were not in their repertoire.

"Wait 'til they get a look at her at the club," Constance said, puckering her mouth in distaste.

"Maybe we should call ahead and ask if they could arrange a hoedown just for tonight," Joanne said.

"She'll be the center of attention, that's for sure," Peter said with a condescending smile. "I just feel sorry for poor Timothy."

We all shook our heads in sad agreement as Roberta joined us.

"Did you show her where she could tinkle?" Constance asked in a little-girl voice and Roberta laughed.

"She raved over every piece of furniture and every toiletry before she tinkled. Her enthusiasm gives me a headache," Roberta said, affecting a weary pose against the bar.

"I can't wait to see her beach ensemble," Joanne said, a definite smirk streaking her face.

"Roberta, you should call the neighbors and charge admission. Make it into a charity event," Joseph said, after downing the rest of his martini and stretching his arm in Peter's direction for a refill.

"Easy does it, partner," Constance said, eyeing her husband with a sudden glint of hostility. "It's only three in the afternoon."

"Yeah, but this is a special event," Joseph responded, flashing his wife a sardonic smile. "We're witnessing the first step in the fall of the House of Monroe." Raising his refilled glass in a mock toast, he hollered, "Today Southampton; tomorrow Hoboken!"

Our streak of black comedy was interrupted a few minutes later by Clare's booming voice as she approached the terrace. "Hello, everybody. I'm ready for my swim."

We all turned to view our new relation with another attack of slack-jaw as we beheld this new apparition.

"What a novel idea: sequins on a bathing suit," Constance said in her hollow imitation of flattery. "Esther Williams would be so jealous."

Indeed, Clare looked like she was ready for the chorus of a Busby Berkly movie water extravaganza—those escapist movies of the thirties where everything was overdone. She was wearing a one-piece bathing suit of a purple satiny material with lots of cleavage, accentuated by sequined flowers outlining both the bodice and her matching bathing cap.

"Simply dazzling!" exclaimed Roberta and unless you were deaf, dumb, blind and severely retarded, you couldn't miss her sarcastic overtone, but Clare seemed to ignore it.

"Thanks," she said, breaking out with a broad smile, showing slightly uneven, grayish teeth—such a contrast, I noted, to the fortune spent by my wife and two sisters-in-law in achieving their perfect plastic smiles. I also noted that while Clare was definitely plump, she still had attractive womanly curves and her legs were good.

"Isn't Timothy going with you?" Joanne asked.

"No, he's taking a nap," Clare explained. "Well, I'm off!"

With this announcement, she kicked off her mules and, with a spirited gait, cantered across the lawn and across the white-sand beach and then, like a life guard on a rescue mission, dove headfirst into the churning surf.

We all watched with fascination as she frolicked in the water, diving in and out of the oncoming waves with all the apparent glee of a child.

"A regular water nymph!" Joseph exclaimed.

"Neptune's daughter!" Joanne added while exchanging smirks with Roberta and Constance.

"Let's have another drink," Joseph said, and we turned back to the bar.

An unusually jovial mood now pervaded our otherwise somber group as we forged a united front of smirking condescension against Clare.

Twenty minutes later, Clare was back on the terrace, wrapped in water, her cap off and her blond hair hanging limply around her cheerful, chubby face.

"That was great!" she exclaimed, reaching for one of the large beach towels that were kept in a stack on the terrace.

"Would you like a drink?" Peter asked.

"Great! How 'bout a Black Russian?"

"I don't think we have the ingredients for that," Peter said patronizingly. "Would you settle for a vodka martini?"

"No thanks," Clare said decisively. "I only like sweet drinks. How 'bout a beer?"

"Foreign or domestic?" Roberta asked archly.

"A good old Bud is fine with me," Clare responded cheerfully, taking no notice of Roberta's airy tone.

"I'm afraid we don't have that label," Peter said, but Roberta jumped in with "I'm sure we must have some in the kitchen. I'm positive I've seen the gardener drinking it."

"Don't go to any trouble," Clare said, massaging her scalp vigorously. "I should take a shower and get ready for dinner."

"We're dining at the club," Peter said.

Clare's eyes sparkled. "Great! Do they have dancing? Timmy and I love to dance."

"There's a small music combo," Peter said. "We'll leave here at six-thirty."

"Great!" Constance hollered, imitating Clare's favorite exclamation. "Can't wait."

"That'll give me time to whip my hair into shape," Clare announced, turning from the group. "See you later."

"Great!" Joseph called after her, as low snickers rumbled across the bar.

* * * *

As we gathered in the foyer before departing for the club, the contrast between Clare and her three sisters-in-law could not have been more dramatic. Tailored dark dresses and sleek conservative hairdos, set off with limited, good jewelry, served as a somber background for

Clare's bright pink, low-cut dress with a ruffled skirt, silver open-toe heels, chunky silver and turquoise necklace matched with chandelier earrings and an assortment of silver bangle bracelets that spread across her arms like some luminous fungus. Her hair had been teased, curled and whipped into another frothy concoction. The overall effect was an exotic Caribbean fruit punch

"Simply stunning!" Constance had announced in an overly dramatic voice as Clare and Timothy descended the stairs toward the rest of the family.

"I'm stunned, too," Joanne quickly said, imitating Constance's dramatic tone.

"Breathtaking! Literally breathtaking!" Roberta exclaimed.

Clare, missing all the nuances, beamed in what she seemed to consider this family circle of admiration. Eyeing all the dark colors adorning her three sisters-in-law, she said, "I like bright colors. They make me feel happy."

"Okay, Cinderella," Joseph said, emboldened by the liquor he had already consumed throughout the afternoon, "then tonight you must feel deliriously happy." Surrounded by phony smiles and a few low snickers, Joseph shouted, "Now it's off to the ball."

* * * *

The club's main dining room was always crowded on a Saturday night—a sea of black, white and gray outfits, offset occasionally by some tastefully colored accessory. As we made our way among the tables to our reserved spot, all eyes turned toward us. Several people called greetings to Peter and Roberta, but most people just stared in dumb disbelief at Clare as she sashayed across the room, smiling or, as she might say, casting great beams of happiness at everyone.

Not since the charity show last fall when the men had dressed as chorus girls, had anyone seen anything like this. Actually, she could have been mistaken for a drag queen. If the Queen of England had suddenly appeared wearing her imperial crown, a grass skirt and army combat boots, she would not have attracted more astonished attention than Clare.

Roberta, Constance and Joanne wore amused, knowing looks that said to all, *we know she's ridiculous and we find her as funny as you do, so we brought her here for your amusement.* Yet a little twitch in my wife's left cheek was the tell-tale sign to me that she was not altogether certain that she should even be seen in Clare's company, no matter how striking the difference in their appearance and demeanor.

We were barely seated and a round of drinks ordered—Clare got her black Russian—when the five-piece band struck up a lively fox trot.

"Oh, Timmy, let's dance," Clare said with genuine excitement. Without hesitating she was out of her seat and headed for the small dance floor, with Timothy dutifully in tow. All heads now once again swiveled in her direction as she began to dance. Mesmerized by her performance, we couldn't turn away.

She wasn't dancing in sync with the music but was always a half-beat off. Her body seemed to break into pieces, with her arms going in one direction, her hips in another, and her feet in a third. She looked like one of Picasso's paintings where the woman's body is disjointed, thrusting out in multiple dimensions. Her eyes were half closed and her face had a far-away look that suggested a trance-like state, like a Sufi circle dancer. The flounces in her skirt flared and dipped and her long necklace whipped around her head like a hula hoop.

Timothy mostly stood in place making conservative movements with his hips and occasionally establishing brief contact with Claire as she gyrated around him like a whirling dervish.

When the fox trout ended, the band, as if sensing that they had an uninhibited exhibitionist on their hands, immediately started a rumba. Without pausing for a breath, Clare didn't so much shift rhythms as increase the tempo off her gyrations and the undulations of her hips. I noticed that Timothy had a broad, indulgent smile on his face.

I heard a man at the next table say, "The best floor show I've seen in years," and the woman sitting next to him added, "She could bring back vaudeville."

The three wives at our table watched Clare's performance with raised eyebrows and bemused smiles. It occurred to me that they probably felt so secure in their social positions that they could introduce this carnival performer to their crowd without any fear of being tarnished, themselves—the way they hired clowns for children's parties or belly dancers at husbands' birthday parties. They were exchanging glances and nods, not only with each other but with their many friends and acquaintances around the room, as if to say, *we know she's ridiculous.* Still, that little twitch in my wife's left cheek revealed a lack of certainty as to how this would all be taken.

The few couples who had taken to the dance floor with Clare and Timothy had either returned to their tables or stopped and were standing in an informal circle, watching this spectacle. Oblivious to everything, Clare seemed tireless as she continued her ecstatic terpsichorean solos across the dance floor. Timothy barely changed tempo, no matter what the dance, but no one noticed, for Clare was the cynosure of all eyes and clearly the subject of most comments. Only when the band took a short break did Clare and Timothy return to our table, beads of sweat dotting Clare's cleavage and her elaborate hairdo slightly askew.

"Oh, that was great!" Clare announced, wiping her forehead with her napkin. "Timmy and I just love to dance. It was one of the first things that brung us together." Timothy patted his wife's arm and gave her an indulgent smile.

The three wives now went into high gear.

"We can see you're a natural," Joanne said.

"You should give lessons," Roberta suggested in an overly sincere voice

"Don't you dance?" Clare asked Roberta.

"Yes, but not with the originality you display. You're in a class by yourself."

"I just let the music take over me and go with the flow," Clare explained in a semi-rapturous tone.

"That's your special gift," Constance said, equaling Roberta's false note of sincerity. "You can't duplicate that."

Intermittently, through two rounds of drinks and a four-course dinner, Clare, with seemingly inexhaustible energy, dragged Timothy back to the dance floor where she never disappointed her dazzled audience. But if her performance on the dance floor was spectacular, her performance at the table was equally noteworthy.

While the other wives ordered salmon with mixed vegetables, salad with vinaigrette dressing on the side and no dessert, Clare couldn't find anything on the menu that she didn't like. She finally settled on rack of lamb, mashed potatoes, creamed spinach, salad "with lots of blue cheese dressing, please," and for dessert, a concoction called "Over The Top" consisting of an oversized brownie topped with mounds of ice cream, chocolate sauce and whipped cream. I privately ventured a guess that no woman in the history of this club had ever ordered that dessert before. The astonished look on the waiter's face when Clare made her selection, confirmed my theory.

"Ladies, you all eat like birds," Clare said, as she contentedly licked the last bit of whipped cream from her spoon. "You left at least half of everything you ordered on your plates. You should put some meat on them bones."

The eyebrows of all three wives immediately soared up to their hairlines and I could tell that this was all-out war.

Constance was first with the dagger. "You're blessed with a lumberjack's appetite. We're all not as fortunate."

Joanne followed, with an icy stare. "You've eaten enough for all of us. I feel like I've gained five pounds just watching you."

Roberta brought up the rear and gave the dagger an extra twist. "If I ate like you, Clare, I'd have to hurry on down to Lane Bryant for a whole new plus-size wardrobe. You'd have to help me pick out *happy* colors."

Clare put her dessert spoon down and smiled. "Well, that's an honest opinion, anyway," she said with no trace of rancor. "I guess we just come from two different worlds."

"You think?" Constance said quickly, but Clare continued smiling and said, "I love to eat and Timmy loves me as I am, so it's a win-win deal for me."

The highlight of the evening came after dinner when the band played a set of Beatles songs that allowed Clare to really cut loose. Her hip-swinging, pelvic-thrusting, breast-heaving, arm-waving, head-bobbing, hand-clapping, foot-stomping maneuvers quickly cleared the dance floor, as people stood around again, awed by this uninhibited display encompassing every dance known to man from ancient tribal rituals to Katherine Dunham and Chubby Checkers.

The spontaneous applause that erupted at the end of this dancing orgy was, I saw, filled with smirking condescension, but Clare was smiling broadly and nodding her head as though in grateful acknowledgment of her audience's admiration, as she made her triumphal progress back to our table.

"Bravissima!" Peter shouted, joining the crowd in their mock display of adulation.

"You really outdid yourself," Constance said.

"An unforgettable display of all your talents!" Roberta added.

"I'll certainly never forget it," Joanne chirped.

I thought that all this phony praise was getting much too heavy- handed but Clare seemed to accept everything at face value and was beaming. Timothy said he was going out for a breath of air and I went with him.

No sooner had we passed through the French doors onto the terrace when Timothy turned to me with eyes blazing.

"You think I don't know what's going on here?" he asked, his voice low and intense.

"What?" I said stupidly, unprepared for this ambush.

"Those three bitches have been having a field day, mocking Clare from the moment she arrived, and my dear brothers are joining in the fun."

Timothy's jaw was twitching and his eyes bored into mine. I struggled to mount a reasonable defense.

"Timothy, you have to admit that Clare is very different from Stephanie, or any woman you ever dated, for that matter. We're just surprised, that's all."

"So you think you can take cheap shots at her because, unlike you sophisticates, she takes everyone at face value and doesn't see the snide, snickering comments you're showering on her?" In a totally unexpected gesture, Timothy grabbed the lapels of my jacket and moved his face to within an inch of mine, as his words exploded. "You know something: for all your fucking sophistication, you're really very provincial because you can't accept anyone who isn't in your milieu or just as phony as you are!"

"You're not being fair," I stammered, stalling for time and realizing that we had been a bit shitty. "She's very different from what we expected and we just have to get used to her."

"Bullshit!" Timothy shouted, then continued in a lower voice. "Your wife and the other two bitches would never accept her, and I'll tell you why: because she's her own unique person. She's real and honest and open and spontaneous—all the things my brothers' wives are not and never could be because they're only interested in their wealth and status and looks and pretending to enjoy people and have a good time, when in reality everything is pretense and calculation with them. They can never relax and just have a good time because they're consumed with what others think of them."

Timothy was cutting loose with a lot of pent-up anger; yet I had to admit that he wasn't far off the mark about Constance and Roberta and my wife, too. He let go of my lapels and moved a short distance away. Now he spoke in a lower, less heated tone.

"I'll tell you something, Mark. After Stephanie starved herself to death because she didn't want to get fat, get old, and lose her competitive edge, I was thoroughly sick of all the games most women play and I wasn't looking for anything with a woman except sex. Then I met Clare, and I had the same first impression you did: gaudy, glitzy, vulgar and shameless, with her best years clearly behind her. I wasn't even interested in giving her a toss in the hay, except I got drunk that first night we met at a party and she was the only one left to drive me home. She put me to bed and slept in the guest room and had breakfast ready for me when I got up the next morning. Then we talked. We talked the whole morning. She asked me questions about my work and she really listened, and when she didn't understand something, she'd freely admit it. There was something so warm and genuine and guileless about her that just drew me in. More in gratitude than anything else, I took her to dinner that night and discovered her honesty and uninhibited nature."

Timothy paused and for the first time since we had arrived on the terrace, a small smile crinkled the sides of his mouth. He gazed off in the distance as though conjuring up a scene.

"Clare had ordered a half-melon as an appetizer and she dipped her spoon in the melon like a battering ram, and a wedge of melon flew into the air like a projectile and landed on the dress of a lady at the next table. An embarrassing scene for anyone, right? Not for Clare! She jumped up and went right over to the lady and picked the melon wedge off her shoulder and made a loud apology. Then she returned to our table and continued to eat her melon as if nothing unusual had happened. At that moment I knew she was special." Timothy paused, took a deep breath, and returned his gaze to me.

"Mark, I never met anyone who loves life more than Clare does. She gets a kick out of the littlest things. She makes me happy in ways I could never imagine. Yes, I know the impression she has on people and, no, I don't give a damn Her grammar is atrocious; her sense of style is strictly trailer park; and she doesn't know which fork to use. So what! She's taught me not to care about what other people think and that's a sense of freedom you can't believe. It's such a release! I've never known such freedom and happiness...such love. And I have no desire to change her; to mold her into something akin to all the other women we've known, for fear she would become self-conscious and lose all that marvelous spontaneity I adore."

Timothy shifted his gaze back toward the dining room.

"But I don't want to see her hurt, and those witches in there are shifting into high gear, so before I lose my cool and we have an all-out family melee, you'd better get the word out to tone it down. We'll be gone tomorrow and they'll never have to see her again. I only came because she wanted to meet my family. Not having any of her own, she thinks families are a big deal."

Another smile flashed across Timothy's face. "Anyway, Mark, I'm sorry to make you the brunt of all my anger." Timothy gave me a playful slap. "As my kid brother you were always my punching bag, remember?"

He feigned a couple of jabs to my ribs and we both laughed. I was relieved that his anger had abated but saw the potential danger in any further snide remarks from the ladies and was determined to get the word out. We headed back to the others.

Without going into details, as we were getting ready for bed that night I suggested to Joanne that she and the others should cut out the sarcasm. Sitting at her dressing table with gobs of cream smeared over her face, she raised one eyebrow and said, "The cow is too stupid to get our little jokes so I wouldn't worry."

"Still," I said, "Timothy gets them and doesn't like it one bit. Just go easy tomorrow."

Joanne interrupted her nightly beauty ritual to wave her hand dismissively in my direction. I went into the bathroom to brush my teeth. When I returned, Joanne was already in bed, with hair curlers, chin strap and sleep mask all in place, projecting the allure of a Komodo dragon. *No wonder our sex life went south*, I thought as I climbed into bed. Then, with rising jealousy, I began fantasizing about the love life of Timothy and the uninhibited Clare. Vivid images in my fevered imagination seemed to spill over into my dreams that night, with body parts rapturously gyrating in all directions.

The next day there was a catered barbecue on Peter's rear terrace. Since both front and rear terraces were broad enough for commercial planes to land on, the rear terrace was used for such occasions as this because of its superb ocean view.

Once again, Clare appeared in another gaudy outfit with an abundance of accessories, and, once again, the three other wives made not-so-subtle cutting remarks that seemed to sail completely over Clare's head. She was too busy raving about the food, the color of the sky, the majestic waves and even the beautiful lawn.

Before departing for the city and a flight back to California, Clare pronounced everything as having been "great" and invited us all to visit them next year "or sooner if you're in the neighborhood."

"I'd rather have a root canal," Joanne muttered between the parted teeth of her frozen smile as we all stood on the front terrace, waving them off.

"Well, wasn't that a memorable experience!" Roberta said, clearly weary from all her forced jollity, as she walked back into the house, the rest of us trooping after her.

"Let's have another drink," Joseph suggested, avoiding his wife's disapproving frown as he headed for the bar. We followed him.

* * * *

As Roberta observed, it was a memorable experience, for that was the last weekend that all of us were together. In the fall of that year Peter divorced Roberta and shortly thereafter married a leggy model, twenty-two years his junior. The following winter my brother Joseph was hospitalized for severe alcohol poisoning. He came through that and joined AA. He also found Jesus, was born again like George W. Bush, and separated from Constance, claiming their life goals were no longer compatible.

Joanne and I muddled on for another three years until, bone weary, we agreed to call it quits. She didn't take me to the cleaners as I had predicted because she already had another guy—a hedge-fund big shot—lined up to take my place. I've had short-term relationships since my divorce that never developed into anything meaningful. The ghosts of my ex-wife and my former sisters-in-law always rose up and seemed to take possession of my latest girlfriend—a gesture, an artful pose, a suspicious look, a cutting remark, a lie—and I would gradually lose interest.

I found myself drawn to Timothy and Clare during these upended times, and I'd visit them in California once or twice each year.

The home Clare had made for Timothy was warm, cluttered, relaxed and fun. People were dropping in all the time and were always welcome. Parties and outings were mostly spontaneous and the gaiety seemed real. Their home was just a few blocks from the beach and Clare swam in the ocean most every day. I can see her still, bobbing, dipping, jumping, diving and laughing— always laughing—with some gaudy cap covering her head, gleaming like a beacon among the churning waves.

Clare's unique personality went unnoticed among the literary and artistic crowd that surrounded her and Timothy, where eccentricity was the norm, and all standards, and no standards, were accepted. Timothy's literary clients all loved his wife, so in his line of work she was a definite asset.

"You and Timothy certainly have a good life," I commented to Clare one night as we sat alone on the patio of their home while Timothy was inside taking a phone call from a client. "I envy you."

Clare became unusually quiet as she gazed up at the night sky. Finally she spoke in a somber voice. "I told Timmy after we spent that weekend with all of you that those were three of the unhappiest women I had ever met and I didn't see how their marriages could last."

"You mean you caught all their phoniness?"

Clare looked directly at me and smiled. "Honey, I catch a lot of things that I choose to ignore. Life's too short."

My admiration for my sister-in-law grew tremendously with that surprising revelation.

A group of friends would frequently join Clare and Timothy at a local club that had dancing. Clare would be in ceaseless motion, never tiring and insisting on dancing with every man in our group. Gradually, I learned to be like Timothy and just stand in one spot, tapping my feet, occasionally shifting my hips and pointing with my arms toward my gyrating partner as she swirled, spun and swiveled around me. Never quite in sync with the tempo and always in a suspended state of intense pleasure, she danced to a rhythm all her own, and I wished, hoped—and sometimes even prayed—that someday I could be like that.

See No Evil

A small article in a supplementary section of the *Sunday Times* titled "Closing of a Landmark" caught Mr. Henry Clay's attention by chance. He read the first sentence as long-dormant, unbidden thoughts stirred his memory

"The Thoughtful Reader bookstore, for more than six decades a landmark on Manhattan's West 96 Street, will, to the disappointment of its small, devoted clientele, soon be gone."

The article went on to say that the Lowe family had been the only proprietors since Mr. Jonathan Lowe had opened the store in 1946, shortly after returning from WW II. The store was now operated by his son, Justin. A new owner had bought the building housing the bookstore on the street level and planned to renovate the entire five-story structure. When notice was given of a doubling of the rent, Justin was quoted as saying, "We could barely meet the current rent," and, reluctantly, the store would close in three months at the end of its current lease.

A few more lines detailed the death of small, individual bookstores, leaving only the mega-chains. The article ended with quotes from book lovers lamenting the loss of the idiosyncratic stores where, amidst the jumble of old and new books, esoteric authors and surprising, arcane subjects could be found. One disappointed customer was quoted as saying, "Going to Barnes & Noble just isn't the same experience as browsing in The Thoughtful Reader. That's like comparing MacDonald's to a fine old restaurant."

Henry Clay finished the article and, quickly putting the paper down on his lap, stared fixedly into space. The morning light from the wide windows of his Manhattan penthouse apartment illuminated his pensive expression and lent a youthful sheen to his smooth cocoa-brown face, belying his fifty-seven years. Time collapsed as his thoughts raced back to his frequent visits to The Thoughtful Reader, which he had discovered when he was fifteen years old during a tumultuous period in his young life.

Henry Clay's father was unknown to him although he bore his father's last name. When he was thirteen his mother, a crack addict, died of a drug overdose, an event that left Henry confused but not sad since his mother had shown neither love nor solicitude to him or his two younger half-sisters but had kept all three children with her for the welfare checks they brought. Most of this steady income was spent on drugs while her children were denied bare necessities and, at startling young ages, had learned to fend for themselves.

After his mother's death, Henry was placed in a foster home with a black family in Harlem, judged suitable for his own mixed racial background. Here, at least, he received a modicum of attention in terms of being fed regularly and given hand-me-down clothes. But being a bright and sensitive boy, Henry quickly saw that his presence in the household was strictly for the monetary gain he brought, and no emotional sustenance or real concern was ever given. He withdrew into himself, cultivating a callous exterior and a belligerent stance against his indifferent world.

By the time he was fifteen Henry was a frequent truant from school and had discovered a sub-stream of adolescents ranging in age from thirteen to seventeen, all of whom through various circumstances had been discarded by family and detached from society, forming a loose, vagabond brotherhood of the streets. They demonstrated their hostility to the normal social code by dedicating themselves to petty crimes and devious plots, further fueling their bitterness and anomie.

Stealing was their main preoccupation, to which they applied various stratagems. Their most successful scheme was for a few boys to enter a store and stroll about, taking up different positions far away from the counters where the store personnel were. Two boys would then enter the store and pretend to start a raucous fistfight, drawing the full attention of the management. In the few minutes while the employees were focusing on stopping the fight, the other boys would have pilfered pre-selected items and have quickly exited the store, with no one the wiser as to what they had accomplished..

Another gimmick was to enter a store with what appeared to be a tightly wrapped and corded package, which had a false side that could be discreetly opened to transfer items quickly snatched from a counter or display case to the wrapped box under the boy's arm.

Pick-pocketing was a learned skill in which Henry never achieved proficiency and so he played a subordinate role by casually bumping into a selected male victim while another, more adroit member of the gang relieved the man of his wallet. They only practiced this art in the warm months when a bulging back pants-pocket indicated the location of a wallet. Their favorite spot for this sting operation was Central Park West because if the victim quickly discovered his wallet missing, the agile teenagers could be over the wall surrounding the park and disappear in a matter of seconds.

Henry, along with the other loosely-knit gang of teenage street rovers, felt no compunctions about these violations of persons and property, having already, at fifteen, succeeded in walling himself off from all acceptable codes of conduct with hazy notions of exacting revenge on a world that had cast him aside as so much unwanted garbage.

Only one trait separated Henry from the other street kids and contradicted his image as an insensitive tough: he loved to read. This love had been instilled in his first few years of elementary school when he had discovered through the books the teachers read to the class a far-ranging world of fables, fairy-tales, adventures in exotic places and mythical locales, joyful families and happy environments, all alien to anything he had known in his short life and fueling his desire to learn more.

By the second grade he recognized, thanks to the guidance and praise of his teacher, that he was quick in acquiring reading skills; by grade three he was reading independently, thirsting for more books. In the next few years, despite the chaos and deprivations of his home life, with his mother frequently absent or cocooned in a drug haze, he endlessly sought escape through reading, often hiding under his skimpy bedclothes with a flashlight to pursue his passion late into the night. With his mother's death and the subsequent events that confirmed the world's indifference toward him, his desire to read receded into the shadows of his mind as he struggled to cope with his daily existence, his anger and desolation. But this desire, while dormant, was not dead; it re-emerged unbidden at fifteen through a casual circumstance one rainy afternoon in 1970 as he strolled alone down West 96 Street in Manhattan and stopped in front of The Thoughtful Reader bookstore.

A small, weathered shingle hanging above the door, set down three steps from the sidewalk in the lower floor of an old brownstone, modestly proclaimed the store's name. Beside the door a gritty, rain-spotted window displayed not individual books but stacks of them, arranged haphazardly and precariously, some with dust jackets, others naked, their titles faded.

To Henry, suddenly imagining all the knowledge, the flights of fancy, and the different worlds they encompassed, along with the temporary escape from his sordid, shabby world they beguilingly offered, the books were dazzling, an irresistible draw, luring him back to the joys of his early childhood. Acting on impulse fueled by his imagination, he eagerly descended the steps.

Upon entering the store, a musty smell assailed his nostrils, not altogether unpleasant but different from anything he was used to; a commingling of dust, still air, decaying paper and drying glue which he would forever associate with second-hand bookstores. The store was small, narrow and deep. All the walls except for the front wall were covered with bookshelves from floor to ceiling; their shelves sagging from the weight of books crammed at warring angles into every inch of space. On most shelves there were books lying flat in mounds above a bottom row of vertical books—clearly the first-comers—correctly lined with their spines upended.

There seemed to be no clear path or aisles from the front of the store to the rear, and counters, placed with no discernible pattern across the floor, their surfaces covered with uneven piles of books, made browsing an exciting challenge.

At the far corner of the front wall Henry spotted a counter with an old cash register, and, behind more piles of books, he spied a thinning gray- haired head. A small man, appearing to the fifteen-year-old Henry to be old, his complexion mottled and his thin, drooping shoulders covered with a worn cardigan, emerged from behind the counter and offered the boy a warm smile.

"Can I help you, young fella?" he asked in a cheerful tone, his voice striking a reedy pitch.

Henry's larcenous streak, honed to a quick assessment of easy pickings, glanced at the frail looking man who seemed to be the only occupant of the store. Then another, more powerful impulse took over.

"Can I look?" he asked, his eyes darting among the mountains of books, his wonderment fully aroused.

The man's smile broadened, displaying even, discolored teeth.

"Of course! Of course!" he said in a stronger voice. "Look as much as you want. Is there anything in particular you're looking for?"

Thrown momentarily off guard by such an enthusiastic invitation by a white man to a black kid, Henry shook his head, unable to think of an answer. The smiling man continued. "Well, if there's anything I can help you with, just ask. All our books are second-hand so you'll find the prices in pencil on the inside of the cover. It's nice to see a young fella interested in books."

The old man retreated to behind the counter with the cash register and, perching himself on a stool, began reading a book, paying no further attention to Henry.

Silence reigned for a long time in the musty, low-ceilinged bookstore as Henry wondered among the profusion of books piled on the flat wooden counters with scarce space for maneuvering among them. He felt a calm peacefulness, alien to the tumult and heightened vigilance that pervaded his everyday life; yet, he also felt an opposite surge of excitement as he read hundreds of titles in what was clearly a selection of history books dealing with Rome, Greece, Colonial America, the Civil War and various empires he couldn't even place in any chronological order: the British Empire, Byzantine Empire, Mogul Empire, Spanish Empire, Holy Roman Empire.

He had vague memories of hearing some of these names during his spotty years in noisy, overcrowded classrooms where distractions were numberless and learning was not his priority. Here, for the first time he felt a compelling desire to learn about them.

He ambled among the counters, coming eventually to one that contained an assortment of fictional works and spotted a title that he happily recognized: *A Christmas Carol* by Charles Dickens. He had found a tattered paperback copy with this title a few years ago on top of some garbage as he strolled aimlessly in his neighborhood, looking for action. He had walked to a small, scruffy park and sat on a bench with half the slats missing and started reading. Hours passed and he sat motionless, immersed in the story of Ebenezer Scrooge, Tiny Tim and the ghosts. Some of Dickens' vocabulary—words he had never heard spoken by anyone—caused him to stumble, but the plot, the vivid characters and the sentiment kept him enthralled.

The natural light was fading when he had finished the book and he had walked home still enveloped in the Dickens' world, temporarily escaping his own sordid life and experiencing a buoyant spirit of joyfulness. His buoyancy disappeared upon reaching home and learning that his mother had been taken to a hospital where she died the next day. The pleasures of reading quickly faded as he plunged into the sordid maelstrom of his fractured life.

Now, as he stood in this bookstore, gazing at the same title, a surge of excitement shot through him. He wanted not only to read the magical story again but felt an irresistible compulsion to possess this hardcover book lying before him.

He glanced over at the frail man and saw his head still bowed over his book, seemingly oblivious to his one customer. The temptation was too great for Henry. With one swift motion he leaned across the counter as if peering at another title while his hands deftly deposited *A Christmas Carol* inside his jacket. He wanted to escape safely with his spoils and started walking toward the door. From behind him he heard a voice.

"Can I help you?"

Henry turned abruptly to see a tall, stocky young man in his twenties standing in an open doorway at the back of the store. Past the young man's silhouette Henry spied more stacks of books in what appeared to be a storage room. Momentarily flustered, Henry regained his bravado with a sharp "No." The young man had a look on his face that Henry saw as challenging, as if he had been standing in the doorway long enough to see Henry swipe the book. Henry was about to bolt for the front door when he heard the older man's voice.

"It's alright, Justin. The fella's just looking."

"Yes, I'm just lookin," Henry echoed with a defiant glint in his eyes.

Justin offered a slight nod but his expression was enigmatic and Henry was on guard. The older man came from behind his counter and approached Henry, whose eyes flickered from the approaching man to the entrance, still uncertain what was about to happen and ready to bolt.

"Did you find anything interesting?" the older man asked with a warm smile that put Henry at ease.

"Nah," Henry said nonchalantly, then added "I gotta go."

"Well, you be sure to come back and see us," the older man said, making a sweeping motion to take in all the book-laden counters. "I like a fella who's interested in books."

Henry glanced back at Justin who was still standing behind him with that slight smile that Henry could almost swear was a sneer.

"You didn't finding anything that interested you?" Justin asked, his voice rising at the end of his question, conveying doubt or suspicion, Henry couldn't decide.

"That's what the fella said, Justin," the older man cut in quickly, while withdrawing a card from the pocket of his worn cardigan and offering it to Henry. "By the way, what's your name?"

Still on full alert Henry was surprised by the older man's question and, momentarily taken in by the warm, crinkly smile, he said, "Henry," careful not to give a last name.

"You come back now, Henry."

Henry glanced down at the card: The Thoughtful Reader, Jules Lowe, Proprietor.

"Thanks," he said over his shoulder while making a hasty exit.

* * * *

Henry read *A Christmas Carol* again with the same transporting delight he had experienced the first time, only now he found extra excitement in looking at the embossed leather cover and the slightly faded gold lettering, knowing that he possessed this treasure, that it was his and his alone. He hid it in a cardboard box under the metal cot where he kept his few clothes and a faded picture of his mother as a pretty, smiling young woman before she descended into her private, despairing hell. The cot with its starving mattress and the scant floor space beneath it were the only territories he could claim as his, in the dark, crowded apartment of his foster family.

A few weeks after his first visit, Henry felt an overwhelming urge to return to The Thoughtful Reader.

Again the inexplicable desire to possess books as things that he alone could savor and take pride in owning came over him. Even with the suspicious frown of the young man called Justin still looming in his memory, he concluded that the bookstore could be easy pickings for his skills of deception and legerdemain, and back to the bookstore he went. This time he carried a wrapped package with a false side that could easily accommodate two or three books and wore a jacket with large inner pockets.

The frail older man was again perched on a stool behind the counter with the cash register and again engrossed in reading a book when Henry entered the store as a small bell with a hollow whimper announced his presence. The man looked up and a broad smile creased his face.

"Well, hello there, young fella. Welcome back," he said in a voice conveying exuberance seemingly at odds with his frail frame. "It's Henry, right?"

Involuntarily, Henry dropped his guard and responded with his own smile, touched by the warm personal greeting. "Right," he said while surveying the scene. He spotted two customers but no Justin.

"Where's the young guy?" he asked quickly, then felt that his question would arouse suspicion. The man continued smiling.

"Oh, you mean my son. He's making a delivery,"

"A delivery?"

"Yes. We have a lady who's been a long-time customer but now she's confined to her apartment so she calls up and orders a bunch of books at a time and Justin delivers them."

Henry nodded, pleased that he wouldn't have to deal with Justin this time.

"Anything special you're looking for?"

Before thinking, Henry blurted out, "What you got by Charles Dickens?"

The man chuckled. "We've got lots of copies of Dickens' novels. You'll find some in the fiction counter over there," he said, pointing to the general area where Henry had found *A Christmas Carol*. "And there's a lot more on the shelves along the back wall."

Henry nodded. The old man returned to his reading and Henry moved toward the back of the store. He found several shelves containing the collected works of Dickens and was amazed to see how many books Dickens had written. Instantly he wanted to possess them all. He kept an eye on the two other customers. When one customer went to the counter to purchase a few books and was engaged in an animated conversation with the man, Henry saw his chance. The second customer was near the front of the store with his back to Henry.

Henry took a leather-bound Dickens book off one of the groaning shelves. The title was *Oliver Twist*. He liked the sound of that name. After another furtive glance around the store, he slipped the book into the false side of the package he carried under his arm. Emboldened by this successful maneuver, he selected another title, *David Copperfield*, and that, too, went into the package. Finally, in quick succession, he selected a third book, *Great Expectations*, and now this choice was safely hidden in the package. He rearranged the remaining books, hoping to conceal the gaps left by the three stolen copies and decided to leave rather than press his luck by sliding a few more into the interior pockets of his jacket.

The frail man was still chatting with the lady by the cash register but interrupted his conversation to call out, "Come and see us again, Henry."

Henry's pulse was racing but he managed a nod as he hastened out the door and up the three steps to the street where he quickly melded with the sidewalk crowd.

In the next few weeks, Henry consumed his newly acquired treasures and then deposited them in the cardboard storage box under his cot. The compulsion to own more books again overtook him. Telling himself that neither the frail man, Mr. Lowe, nor his son, Justin, would miss the books he had swiped, he boldly returned to The Thoughtful Reader, package under his arm, for another foraging expedition.

As soon as he entered the store he was disappointed to see Justin behind the check-out counter. Justin saw him and his expression became a scowl. "Just browsing some more?" he asked in a clearly challenging tone.

"Maybe," Henry shot back defiantly, but he decided instantly that he would not attempt any book stealing today since he knew Justin would be watching him closely. He decided to spend a few minutes sauntering among the counters and then make a hasty exit. He followed this plan and was about to leave when Mr. Lowe appeared from the back room.

"Hello Henry," he called in his thin, cheerful voice, and Henry turned and smiled. "Are you leaving so soon?"

"I gotta go," Henry muttered.

"Wait just a minute," Mr. Lowe said before disappearing into the back room and reappearing moments later. Henry was still standing by the front door, all senses on alert and not knowing what to expect. Mr. Lowe approached him with a book in his hand.

"You seemed interested in Dickens and I have a copy of one of his books with a slightly damaged cover so I thought you might like it."

Mr. Lowe's reference to Dickens made Henry nervous but the man's face was creased in smiling folds with no sign of accusation or suspicion. Henry took the proffered book and read the faded title, *Martin Chuzzlewit.*

He gave Mr. Lowe an awkward "Thanks," and hastily left the bookstore.

For the next several days and nights while Henry devoured Martin Chuzzlewit, his mind was troubled. Mr. Lowe's thoughtful gesture displayed a kindness that Henry had rarely experienced in his life. Now it pricked his conscience, long submerged beneath the anger and alienation with which he defended himself against a hostile world. He knew that he craved more books to read—to own—but he didn't want to continue ripping off this kind man. This troubling conflict weighed on his mind until he hit upon a new scheme.

Cigarettes were a hot commodity among his peers. He would steel packs of cigarettes from various stores and sell them at a discount to other kids on the street; thereby earning money to allow him to be a legitimate customer of Mr. Lowe's and *buy* books at his store. He put his new plan into effect the next day. It was easy for him to pilfer packs of cigarettes from many different stores. In two weeks he had ten dollars and change when he again returned to The Thoughtful Reader.

Now, as a potential paying customer he was happy to see Justin by the cash register, but shortly after he entered, Mr. Lowe emerged from the storage room and gave him a warm greeting before turning to his son.

"Justin, there's some unfinished work in the back that I'd like you to attend to."

Justin scowled, looked at Henry, then back at his father. He said nothing and disappeared into the storage room. Mr. Lowe took his usual place on the stool behind the check-out counter.

"Call if you need any help," he said genially before burying his nose in a book.

Henry headed for the back shelves with the various second-hand sets of Dickens, feeling a surging pride that this time he could buy something. After looking over the titles, he selected a book bound in green leather titled *The Old Curiosity Shop* and saw the price marked three dollars. Elated that he could buy another book, from the same leather-bound set he selected *Dombey & Son*, which was also marked three dollars. Euphoria gripped him as he selected a third title, *Pickwick Papers*, also marked three dollars, and proudly carried his selections to the check-out counter.

Mr. Lowe glanced up from his book as Henry deposited his selections on the crowded counter. An unmistakable look of surprise and delight swept across the frail man's face.

"I'm a Dickens lover, too," he exclaimed as he rang up the price of each book on the ancient, ornate cash register. "What draws you to his books?"

Henry's brow furrowed as he struggled for an answer, but Mr. Lowe's encouraging smile reduced the boy's self-consciousness.

"I like the people in his stories and how they struggle against a lot of shit—I mean, a lot of obstacles—to make somethin' of themselves. Some of the people are funny and some are sad and some are really fuckin' cruel—I mean, cruel—and they all live in England in another time that's very different from our time here but there's still a lot of crap that we're still facing today like poverty and sufferin' and the break-up of families and the rich gettin' over on the poor."

Henry abandoned any further comments with a defeated shrug.

"I don't know. I just like the way he writes and describes people and places and all the wonderful words he uses."

The broad smile never left Mr. Lowe's face as he listened attentively to Henry's remarks, nodding his head in agreement.

"Good for you," he said as Henry stared down at the counter, frustrated by not being able to put into adequate words the magical times he spent transported to a different world where goodness usually triumphed over adversity and even among the lowest people—society's outcasts—love and friendship were delicate threads soothing and connecting them.

"Dickens is a master at describing his characters and creating interesting plots, as you say," Mr. Lowe said cheerfully. Henry flashed a smile, pleased that Mr. Lowe was affirming his struggling thoughts.

"By the way, Henry, we have a policy here that when you buy three books, you get a fourth one free. Would you like to select another Dickens title?"

Henry felt a quickened excitement at the prospect of acquiring another book and was digesting this offer when he heard Justin's loud voice exploding behind him. "Dad!"

The smile left Mr. Lowe's face and his eyes shifted to his son. "Justin, please stay out of this," was all he said in a stern voice.

"But Dad!" Justin bellowed.

"Get back to your work!" Mr. Lowe responded in an unconditional tone.

"Jesus!" Justin exclaimed as he turned and disappeared into the back room.

Mr. Lowe resumed his smile, turning his full attention to Henry.

"That's nine dollars plus tax, Henry, and don't forget to select a fourth book."

Henry dug into his jacket pocket and produced worn dollar bills, quarters, nickels and dimes, grandly depositing this assortment on the counter. His expression reflected great satisfaction. Mr. Lowe counted aloud the seven dollar bills and then the change until the nine-dollars-plus-tax total was reached. He deposited this amount in the cash register as Henry scooped up the remaining change.

"I think you might like *Nicholas Nickleby*," Mr. Lowe called out as Henry headed for the back shelves. He quickly found that title in the same green leather binding and returned to the check-out counter. Mr. Lowe deposited all four books in a paper bag.

"I almost forgot," he said, reaching under the counter and producing a worn paperback. "I have too many copies of this book. It's very different from Dickens, much more contemporary, but I think you might like it. It's about a youngster around your age who's struggling to come to terms with all the hypocrisy and phoniness he sees around him. It's called *Catcher In The Rye*."

Mr. Lowe dropped the paperback into the bag with the four Dickens novels and, still smiling broadly, handed the bag to Henry.

"Be sure to let me know what you think of all these new books," he said.

"Thanks. I will," was all Henry could say, but his mind was already crowded with wonderful speculations about the contents of this newly acquired collection as he left the store and leapt up the three steps, barely able to contain his happiness, exulting in an alien joy of Mr. Lowe's kindness.

And so began a new phase in Henry Clay's life, unfolding gradually but perceptibly over time. He spent fewer days on the streets running with packs of disaffected teenagers and more time lying on his cot—the only place he could claim as his own—reading. The foster family with whom he shared space—but not his life—had no interest in books and regarded his new habit as peculiar but, in total indifference, left him alone. He discovered the library in his run-down school and, despite its meager collection, he managed to find books on history and science fiction and more classics that captured his interest.

It was as though some interior spigot of endless curiosity had suddenly been turned on and out poured an insatiable thirst for information about the world, the way it was, the way it had been and the way it might be in the future. Above all, Henry Clay fell in love with words, their nuanced meaning, their power, their sound. There was an old battered copy of an oversized dictionary on a wobbly stand in the school library where he could usually be found during his lunch break busily shuffling its pages and copying a word's definition in a notebook that he now carried everywhere.

His attendance at school shot up and teachers noticed a quiet intensity that Henry had never exhibited before. Remarkably, he seemed genuinely interested in what they had to say, and this new, focused earnestness was rewarded with improved grades. His stunned teachers happily noted that his writing had taken on a descriptive fluidity and attempts at artful phrasing—sometimes stilted and occasionally archaic but revealing a subtle intelligence and a creative drive. Thanks to the recommendation of the school librarian, Henry had discovered the public library and became a frequent visitor.

Throughout this extended period, Henry always returned to The Thoughtful Reader eager to share his ideas and reading responses and even his academic achievements with Mr. Lowe who always showed a keen interest in his continuing progress as a reader. No longer did he ever consider stealing books, for a major attitudinal shift had occurred: his original desire to physically possess books had now been supplanted by his craving for possessing the knowledge they contained. More importantly, he relished the discussions he would have about the books with Mr. Lowe. Justin continued to regard Henry with a wary eye but over time he seemed resigned to the teenager's visits and chats with his father.

Mr. Lowe always found some excuse to give Henry a free book on each of his visits but soon Henry was returning the book after reading it. Under Mr. Lowe's casual tutelage Henry discovered Hemingway, Steinbeck and Fitzgerald who, along with Dickens and Salinger, became his favorite authors.

Beyond the fascinating books with their shimmering words, unique phrasing and insights into the human spirit, and beyond the chats with Mr. Lowe that fostered deeper, richer reflections on the quality of each author's writing and the astute dissection of character and personality, Henry returned to The Thoughtful Reader because he found in Mr. Lowe a man who, in myriad thoughtful ways, cared not only about his development as a reader; Mr. Lowe seemed to care about him as a person. For the first time Henry felt valued by another human being whom he respected and wanted to please. An imperceptible, irrevocable bond had formed between the black teenager and the frail Jewish bookseller that was a life line for Henry in nurturing his self-respect.

Several months after the regular pattern of Henry's visits had been established, Mr. Lowe told Henry that business was picking up—a surprise to Henry who had never observed more than a few customers during his many visits—and Justin was making more deliveries as a result of increased phone orders. Would Henry be interested in earning a little spending money by working in the store one afternoon a week, dusting the bookshelves and straightening the books on the counters and sweeping the floor? Henry didn't hesitate in responding, yes.

"Let's say two hours a week at five dollars an hour," Mr. Lowe said cheerfully.

Henry cared more about helping his friend than about the money. The new pattern of weekly visits was quickly established, followed by long chats about books. Delicately, imperceptibly, Mr. Lowe extended the conversations, prompting Henry to talk about his life, his struggles and his dreams. Henry only made oblique references to any regrettable incidents in his shady past, but the general pattern of a life without love or hope was easily discernible to Mr. Lowe, whose intense concentration and benign smiles always encouraged Henry to speak more unguardedly than he ever had before.

The week when he turned sixteen, Henry arrived at The Thoughtful Reader to find the store's interior festooned with balloons and a hand-painted banner saying Happy Birthday, Henry. There was also a birthday cake and two small wrapped presents containing a fountain pen and a brand new leather-bound dictionary. A birthday card had a hand-written note:

"To Henry, a smart boy with a bright future. I look forward to your success. Warmly, Jonathan Lowe."

On reading this message Henry's throat closed and he could only mumble "Thanks," because a wellspring of deep, unsatisfied emotions had suddenly been tapped.

Henry eagerly shared his grade improvements with Mr. Lowe who praised his efforts lavishly. Having been left back a grade because of truancy and total indifference to schooling after his mother died, Henry was now motivated to make up that year by attending summer school He tore through books, finding he had, with consistent application, an abundant memory for facts and a quick grasp of concepts. Even with a double course load his marks rose into the nineties, and he proudly shared his success with Mr. Lowe, both man and boy beaming at each other with unrestrained joy.

"You'll have to start thinking about college soon," Mr. Lowe remarked offhandedly, throwing Henry off his rhythm. If Mr. Lowe had suggested that Henry should fly to the moon, Henry could not have been more surprised, for never had the notion of college entered his world view or been presented as an option for his future. But there is was—a magical, unfolding vista, laid before him by the only person in his life for whom he felt both respect and an emotional attachment.

Henry laughed self-consciously as though dismissing the idea out-of-hand, but a seed had been casually planted deep inside him that would grow and bear fruit beyond his wildest dreams.

The subject of college came up again at the start of Henry's senior year when he met with Mr. Harris, one of the school's several guidance counselors. Mr. Harris, a scrawny, rumpled man with thinning gray hair falling in matted wisps across a mottled forehead shadowing hound-dog eyes and a mouth perpetually set in tired resignation, extracted Henry's file from a large pile of folders on his crowded desk. With robot-like, slow actions, he opened the file and stared at the first page.

Henry had never met this counselor before since he had skipped all previously arranged appointments in past years and had only dealt, reluctantly and belligerently, with the cavalcade of vice principals for discipline, who focused on his truancy, tardiness, failing grades and general rowdiness. Now he sat with his arms folded, vaguely expecting another recitation encapsulating his past misdeeds and indifference.

Mr. Harris brushed some limp hairs from his forehead as he methodically turned the pages in Henry's folder. After several minutes of silence, he looked up with unmistakable surprise disturbing his weary expression. Stabbing the folder with his finger, Mr. Harris said, "You seen to have had a complete conversion. What? Did you find Jesus or something?"

Henry ignored the sarcastic undertone and remained silent, characteristically on guard. Mr. Harris now broke into a slow smile and his tone changed. "You've made a remarkable turnaround in the last year. Your grades have shot up from F's to B's and A's, your attendance has improved to an almost perfect record and you've made up a whole year in summer school."

Mr. Harris turned some more pages in Henry's folder, read some lines and returned his smiling gaze to

Henry. "What's more, several of your teachers now feel that you have a very good mind and real potential. What do you say to that?"

Henry's shoulders relaxed as his lips widened in something between a grin and a smirk, reflecting his uncertainty about receiving any praise except from Mr. Lowe.

Mr. Harris closed Henry's folder and, leaning back in his rickety swivel chair with his hands folded on his lap, asked, "So, now what?"

"What?" Henry repeated, thoroughly confused by the open-ended question.

"What are your plans for after high school?" Mr. Harris asked, a tired tone creeping back into his voice.

"I dunno," Henry replied honestly since thinking about the future had never been part of his mindset, being so immersed in the challenges of his daily life and transfixed in his emotional vacuum.

Mr. Harris leaned forward and quickly checked something in Henry's folder. "You never showed up on any of our testing dates so we don't have any up-to-date records on your current capabilities, but I see here that in junior high school your reading comprehension score was in the ninety-ninth percentile, despite consistently poor or failing grades."

Defensively, Henry shrugged his shoulders.

"I'd like you to take a battery of tests. Will you agree to that?"

Henry silently agreed with a brief nod.

"I'll send word through your teachers on the date and place," Mr. Harris said, writing a quick note on a small pad next to Henry's folder.

Henry made no mention to Mr. Lowe of his meeting with the guidance counselor. He showed up on the appointed day and took the tests that lasted throughout the school hours with a half-hour for lunch. Two weeks later he was summoned to Mr. Harris's cramped, airless office. This time he was met by a beaming, fully animated Mr. Harris as well as a smiling young woman he had never seen.

"Henry, this is Miss Skelly, our outreach coordinator. I've asked her to join me because we have a special situation on our hands."

Instantly, Henry rushed to a judgment of trouble, despite the two smiling faces confronting him, as his long history of antagonistic, demeaning tangles with all manner of social agencies rose up before him with spectral accusations. His face froze in a puckered frown and he was barely breathing.

Mr. Harris continued. "The tests you took show you to have a very high I.Q. as well as strong reading and analytic skills. These place you in the category of gifted."

Henry exhaled deeply as his facial muscles relaxed. Now he gave his full attention to the counselor.

"Until last year, your record was dismal, and that's putting it mildly, but you turned everything around as a junior."

Ms. Skelly, still smiling broadly, interrupted Mr. Harris.

"What caused you to have such a remarkable turnaround, Henry?"

A clouded look overtook Henry. Until that moment he had never considered his change of attitude, his shift in priorities, never given his new life formal recognition. He acted as he felt; he responded to his instincts each day. Now, as he pondered Ms. Skelly's question, Mr. Lowe's benignly smiling face floated into his mind's eye and he recognized and acknowledged the extraordinary influence this gentle man had exercised on him in bringing about a radical transformation.

Henry looked at Ms. Skelly and a slow smile creased his broad face as he crossed his arms and shook his head in an exaggerated gesture of befuddlement. His feelings were too raw and intimate to be shared with a stranger.

Ms. Skelly ignored Henry's baffled response. "If you continue this year to get good grades, I can guarantee that we could find a college placement for you and could look for some financial support, too."

Glimpses of new horizons and expanded vistas now filtered into Henry's thoughts as unexpected possibilities offered a life line of hope. He felt surprisingly giddy with this unexpected affirmation and also energized. Yet, from years of walling off his feelings and guarding his instincts, his spontaneous joy was reflected only in a nodding of his head and a short, nervous spurt of laughter.

That day, that interview, the words said, the future outlined, and the promises made, would be a day of vivid, lasting memory; a day he would replay in his mind through the succeeding decades when faced with challenges of seemingly insurmountable proportions. That day was the lynchpin for the rest of his life: the leap from a junior college to an Ivy League university, the academic honors and generous scholarships, the ever-building momentum to achieve, to excel, to prove his worth.

An M.B.A. with distinction from Harvard launched him on a career where he eventually reached the highest levels of corporate management. Not satisfied with that achievement, he started his own investment company and now, at fifty-seven, a divorced father of thee and a celebrated rags-to-riches billionaire, he turned his attention largely to philanthropic work.

That fateful day with Mr. Harris and Miss Skelly was seared in his mind for another equally compelling reason.

He had rushed from school to share the momentous possibilities of his new future with Mr. Lowe, the only person who meant anything to him, the only person who, he knew, would delight in all these new prospects as vindication of his faith in Henry.

He was crestfallen when he reached the store and found it closed. A handwritten sign hung crookedly in the front window:

"CLOSED DUE TO DEATH OF MR. JONATHAN LOWE, PROPRIETOR. WILL REOPEN SOON."

He vowed never to return to The Thoughtful Reader. That night he retrieved the birthday card from the box of mementoes under his cot and read Mr. Lowe's note. Bewildered and shaken, he crawled into bed and stuffed the pillow over his face. He had never cried for anyone before.

* * * *

The day after reading the Times' article, Henry Clay returned to The Thoughtful Reader. In the four decades since he last saw it, there had been little change to jar his memories. As he opened the door, his senses transported him across time to the day he had first crossed the threshold: the same musty smell with a thin veil of dust notes fluttering in the air; the same exploding piles of books, cascading haphazardly across oddly arranged counters, while the surrounding wall shelves bent ominously from their overload of crammed books. Henry suddenly glimpsed the alienated fifteen-year-old boy—angry, lost, with larceny in his heart—the first time he had entered this store and seen the frail-looking older man, so quick to smile, by the cash register: an encounter that would shift the course of his life.

Henry counted six customers, an unusually high number, he noted, from his many visits so long ago, before turning his attention to the man behind the counter with the same ancient cash register. He studied the man's features, transposing them to the youthful visage of his mind's eye and concluded that this was Justin Lowe who, he calculated, was now in his early sixties. Warily he approached the man and introduced himself, supplying a few details to stir Justin's recollections. Justin, looking quizzical at first, finally nodded in recognition, but the same stern expression that Henry remembered as being Justin's constant response to Henry's presence was now visible once again.

"I read about the store's closing in yesterday's Times," Henry said awkwardly by way of explaining his reappearance after so many years.

Justin nodded, but his expression never changed.

"It's just as I remembered it," Henry added, now regretting his compulsion to return here. "I'm sorry it's closing," he said, rummaging through his mind for

76

something more substantial to say in recognition of Mr. Lowe's influence on his life. 'Your father was very kind to me."

Without changing his expression, Justin responded.

"You probably don't know how kind he *really* was."

A puzzled look swept across Henry's face.

"My father and I knew that you were stealing books from us on your first several visits to the store. I wanted to call the police but my father saw something in you and wouldn't let me. He wanted to encourage your interest in reading and he said that if that was the only way, he could spare the books you were stealing."

Henry listened to Justin's revelations as Mr. Lowe's gentle, smiling face floated before him in contrast to the accusatory stare and resentful tone of his son. Now a softer, almost melancholic look came into Justin's eyes and his voice dipped.

"I've read about you in the papers over the years and I know you're a great success. Up from the streets of Harlem to the highest pinnacles of wealth and all that. I sometimes wonder how much of a role my father played in your transformation and if you give him any credit."

Henry paused before answering in a tone as soft as Justin's but resolute. "Believe me, a great deal."

Now, for the first time, a small smile escaped from the corners of Justin's lips. "I'm happy to hear that," he said quietly. He turned his attention to a woman approaching him with an armload of books. There was nothing more to be said. Henry turned and left the bookshop.

* * * *

Henry returned to his apartment and spent the rest of the day in quiet, intense reflection. Early the next morning, after a restless night, he dialed the home number of Frank Ganon, the man who directed the Henry Clay Foundation, managing all of Henry's philanthropic works.

"Frank, I'm sorry to call you so early—you sound like you're still asleep—but I want to change the direction of our giving and focus on two areas: refurbishing or, if necessary, building new libraries in slum areas, and, second, supporting independent bookstores across the country, especially in poorer neighborhoods."

"What are you trying to be: the Andrew Carnegie of the twentieth-first century?" Frank said in a voice still hoarse from sleep.

"Yeah, something like that," Henry said breezily. "One more thing: I want the libraries to be named after a man I knew, Jonathan Lowe."

"Never heard of him," Frank said.

"Not many people have," Henry replied but offered no further information. "I'll be at your office around ten to go over the details."

Frank agreed and Henry closed his cell phone. In the vast expanse of his two-story library, surrounded with treasured first editions, including multiple sets of Charles Dickens, Henry sat in his favorite leather wing chair, pensive and smiling, as he fingered a tattered birthday card and, for the thousandth time, reread the handwritten words, fading with age but brilliantly clear to him.

Tecla's Bridge

"Why is it," Cora Bristol said, as people were stirring their coffee and Joanne, our hostess, was handing out generous portions of home-made key-lime pie, "that some people from your childhood, no matter how minor a role they may have played in your life at that time, just stick in your memory and seem to haunt you?"

Cora's question caught everyone at the dining table off-guard, coming as it did from out of the blue, since a moment before we had been having an animated discussion about local politics. But because all eight of us were old friends, we took such shifts in conversation in stride and indulged Cora by giving her our full attention. She had seemed somewhat subdued during our entire dinner party and now, as all eyes turned to her, we recognized more fully her pensive mood and gave her reassuring smiles. She gave us a half-smile in return and began to speak.

"Do you remember when we were young and every home had Readers Digest?" she asked evocatively.

Since everyone present was over fifty and five of us had met in college, we nodded affirmatively, and Cora continued.

"I used to love the feature about an unforgettable character and I always wanted to submit a story about my grandmother's best friend, Tecla." She paused and glanced around the table. "Of course, writing isn't my strong suit, so I never did."

"We know, Ms. CPA," Norman said, chuckling.

Cora smiled. "But yesterday I was going through an old family picture album and I came upon a picture of my grandmother and Tecla as young girls back on the farm in Estonia and I was amazed to see how pretty Tecla was, but it wasn't just that. There was something in her look as she smiled for the camera, with her arms around my grandmother; something so open and vibrant and optimistic…just brimming with life and youthful expectations. And then I thought about how her life turned out and it made me sad."

Cora paused and sipped her coffee, but we were hooked.

"Delicious pie, Joanne!" Roger exclaimed and our hostess smiled.

Sally, Roger's wife, added, "No one makes a key-lime pie as good as Joanne's."

Sally was about to say something else but with a wave of his hand Norman silenced her, and we all looked at Cora.

"So how did her life turn out?" Norman asked.

Cora wiped her mouth with her napkin after tasting her pie and murmuring her approval. Another sip of coffee and she began again.

"My grandmother had already married my grandfather and had her first son, my Uncle Peter, when she and my grandfather migrated to America in 1915. They settled in western New York in a small farming community of mostly Estonian immigrants like themselves. From what my grandmother told me when I was a girl, she and Tecla had been very close, really like sisters, which I can understand because my grandmother was the only girl among six brothers."

"Your grandfather must have really been nervous about dating her!" Roger exclaimed and everyone smiled.

"My grandmother was determined to bring Tecla to America. For two years she scoured her farming community for any eligible bachelors, showing a picture of Tecla to them, and one young farmer was instantly smitten and started sending letters to Tecla, written by my grandmother because the farmer could read a little but not write, so he dictated his thoughts to my grandmother and she confessed to me that she embellished them a little. Along with these letters my grandmother would send Tecla her own notes praising this young farmer. After about a year, the farmer proposed and Tecla accepted, delighted to be coming to America, to have found a suitable husband and to be reunited with my grandmother."

"It all sounds wonderful to me," Joanne said. "Anyone for more pie?"

No one accepted since we could sense from the look on Cora's face that this charming story was about to take a turn for the worse and we wanted her to continue.

"Tecla set sail for America, her passage funded by her fiancé, her father and my grandfather. It was 1918, the year of the world-wide influenza epidemic, and by the time she arrived in New York, her fiancé was dead."

General sighs of sympathy rumbled around the table and Cora was quick to add, "But that's not all. In the three years since my grandmother had left Estonia, Tecla had undergone dramatic changes. First, she had been kicked by a horse on her father's farm and had broken her hip. It didn't heal properly and she walked with a pronounced limp. Then her teeth were very bad; several of them had been pulled and the rest were turning black. According to my grandmother, Tecla was acutely aware of her disfiguring teeth and never smiled anymore, giving her an endlessly dour appearance which, coupled with her misshapen hip and serious limp, made everyone in her new community forget that she was only twenty-three and think of her as a sour old maid. She moved into my grandfather's house, sharing a room first with my Aunt Rula, then, years later, with me. She was a terrific worker and helped my grandmother with the housework and her five surviving children. Every morning she'd be up at the crack of dawn with the first crowing of the rooster and she'd be out the door and feeding the chickens and pigs."

"And that was it?" Sally nearly shouted. "That's how she spent the rest of her life?"

"Pretty much," Cora said, surveying the frowning faces, "but don't feel too sorry for her because by the time I came along, she was truly my most unforgettable character."

"How so?" Norman asked.

"Well, as most of you know from those all-night college-dorm sharing sessions, my father died in Korea when I was just three years old. My mother and I were living in Buffalo in 1957 when she met a man who was older than she by about fifteen years. He had his own successful business and liked to spend money and take trips, but he didn't want children around. He proposed marriage but I wasn't included in the package deal, so when I was nine I was shipped off to my grandmother's farm where I shared a room with Tecla. She must have been in her early sixties at the time but to me she looked very old, much older even than my sprightly grandmother, and at first she frightened me."

"This it becoming a gothic novel," Roger said, extending his cup to Joanne for more coffee.

"No," Cora quickly corrected him. "Tecla turned out to be a warm and loving friend. My grandfather had been seriously injured in a tractor accident shortly before I arrived and for the first year that I was there, my grandmother was preoccupied with taking care of him, so I was left pretty much in Tecla's care. She would make my lunch and put me on the school bus in the morning and meet me in the afternoon when the bus dropped me off and we'd walk up the long road to the farmhouse and she'd ask me all about school and then we'd sit in the kitchen and have an afternoon snack together. By the time my grandfather was fully recovered, Tecla and I had formed a strong bond. Then something wonderful happened."

"Tecla fell in love?" Sally asked excitedly.

"My wife is forever the romantic!" Roger said.

"No," Cora said, smiling at her audience.

"Well, don't keep us in suspense, Cora. Tell us!" Joanne insisted, and we all smiled encouragingly.

Cora continued. "My grandmother's teeth started to go bad and she went to a dentist and had most of them pulled and replaced with a bridge. She was very pleased with the shiny white teeth in her new bridge and she insisted that Tecla visit her dentist. Now my grandfather had, for decades, been giving Tecla a small wage for all the work she did, helping both him and my grandmother. Except for buying cloth every few years to make a new dress for Sunday church service, Tecla had few expenses and saved her money. She was very generous to me on my birthday or at Christmas and at other times would occasionally slip me two or three dollars, saying, 'Here. Don't tell anyone.' With a lot of coaxing from my grandmother, Tecla finally agreed to visit the same dentist and after about five visits, Tecla returned to the farm with two new bridges, upper and lower, attached to a few rear molars that the dentist had been able to save."

"And then she fell in love!" Sally shouted, refusing to give up her romantic notion.

"No," Cora said patiently, "but her whole personality changed and she seemed to blossom right before our eyes. Instead of never smiling or, when I told her something funny about a teacher or the kids at school, covering her mouth with her hand when she laughed, now she took great delight in smiling and laughing heartily and she became a sunny extrovert. The following Thanksgiving when my three uncles and one aunt, but not my mother, returned to the farm with spouses and children in tow, they were equally amazed by the change in Tecla's personality, as she played with the children and joked with the grown-ups and even sang an old Estonian folksong after dinner and revealed a beautiful singing voice that no one, except my grandmother, had ever heard before."

"And did she ever fall in love?" Sally asked tenaciously.

"As a matter of fact, Sally, I believe she did," Cora said, happy to satisfy Sally's preoccupation with romance. When I was in high school, my grandmother developed heart trouble that the doctors diagnosed as serious. Tecla took over all of the housework and insisted that my grandmother follow her doctors' orders and get lots of rest. In the afternoon, after I came home from school, I'd visit with my grandmother in her room while she rested. Sometimes I'd read to her and other times she'd tell me about her life, especially the years she spent in Estonia. It was during one of these sessions that she told me, in strict confidence, about Tecla's big romance before she came to America.

"When Tecla was still a teenager she had gone with her parents to attend the funeral of her father's brother in a neighboring village, and there she met a young man. This was all before she was kicked by the horse and developed her limp, so she must have looked like she did in the picture I saw of her and my grandmother: pretty, robust and cheerful. Anyway, this young man was very taken with Tecla but there was a problem. Techla's father had already promised Tecla to the son of the farmer whose land adjoined his. But my grandmother told me that this farmer's son was a big, ugly oaf that no girl in her right mind would want anything to do with. Tecla became moody, and with the coming of spring she started taking long walks by herself in the evening, telling her family she was going to visit my grandmother, who was a young bride at that time, living on her husband's family farm which was a good distance away, but no one thought anything of it since Tecla was a healthy, active teenager. Of course, she wasn't visiting my grandmother most of the time; she was meeting the boy from the neighboring village. My grandmother was too straitlaced to go into details with her sixteen-year-old granddaughter but from hints that she gave, I subsequently came to believe that Tecla became pregnant by this boy before my grandmother left for America. Whatever happened to the baby, if it was born, I don't know, but I think that's why my grandmother and Tecla's family were so eager to get her a new start in life in America."

"That's so sad!" Sally said. 'I wanted Tecla's story to have a happy ending."

"Actually, it does," Cora said with an indulgent smile and nod toward Sally, and we were eager to hear more.

"My grandmother suffered a series of heart attacks over several months and about a year after she had been diagnosed, she suddenly passed away in her sleep. The undertaker came early the next morning and before taking the body away, noticed that my grandmother's teeth were missing. Rather than bothering my grandfather who was in a deep state of shock, the undertaker looked in the bathroom, saw a pair of dentures and took them. After the body was gone, Tecla, who had been comforting my grandfather and me throughout the early morning hours, went upstairs to wash and get dressed. When she came downstairs again I saw that her face was contorted with grief and she seemed sullen and would not speak. She continued in this mood all morning and since I was struggling with my own great sense of loss, I left her alone.

"The day passed in silence and the next morning my grandfather, Tecla and I went into town to the funeral parlor to see my grandmother's body before the viewing hours began. We approached the open casket and I was shocked. This was not the serene, pretty lady I had kissed goodnight just a short time ago. Her cheeks were puffy and she had a decidedly petulant look around the mouth. Mr. Early, the undertaker, was standing behind us and I turned to him with a look of total distress. 'We had difficulty with her dentures,' he explained quickly and I looked back at my grandmother's distorted face.

"Tecla's hand touched my shoulder and when I turned to face her, she was smiling a lopsided smile and I saw that her dentures were suspended in mid-air inside her mouth. Than I realized what had happened. 'There's been a mistake, Mr. Early,' I explained hastily. 'You took the wrong dentures!' Mr. Early looked at Tecla who was still displaying her ill-fitting teeth and instantly understood. He offered Tecla his handkerchief and she turned away from us and deposited her teeth in it, folded it neatly and handed it back to Mr. Early. 'Just give me a few minutes, please,' Mr. Early said.

"We moved out into the hall and Mr. Early closed the door to the room where my grandmother's body lay. About fifteen minutes later, the door opened and we trooped back in to see my grandmother and the transformation was remarkable. Mr. Early now handed his handkerchief again to Tecla. 'I had them cleaned,' he said, and she moved to the rear of the room and when she returned, she was both crying and smiling."

"Is that the happy ending you promised us?" Sally asked, clearly disappointed.

"No," Cora said, and took a sip of what was now her cold coffee. "This is!"

Sally leaned forward expectantly and we all listened.

"All three of us returned to the farm and a year later I was graduated from high school and went off to college and, except for periodic visits, I never lived there again. But Tecla and my grandfather lived on for another sixteen years, remaining on the farm together with only a young hired hand for help. Each time I returned to see them, Tecla seemed to glow with happiness and although my grandfather became more crotchety with age, he, too, seemed very pleased with his domestic arrangement."

"Love blooms at any age!" Sally shouted exultantly. We laughed

"On my last visit before his death my grandfather complained that Tecla was quite batty. He told me how at night she would get up and go outside with a flashlight and stand in the front yard and she'd aim the light at the sky and when he found her there one night and asked her what she was doing, she said she was guiding the alien spaceships into the open field. But he chuckled when he told me this story and I really believe that they were good companions in their old age. Besides, I noticed that Tecla's room—the one I had shared with her—was closed off and she had moved into my grandfather's room."

"Okay, then that's the great ending I was hoping for," Sally said, waving her arms in jubilation.

"I'm afraid not," Cora said, as her facial expression changed to a more somber look. "Tecla survived my grandfather by four years, inherited the farm and stayed there until her death from cancer. I was with her when she was dying. It was a slow, painful death and she was in and out of consciousness, mumbling one minute and shouting something the next. Her last words were 'My baby…my baby! Don't take my baby!'"

Silence fell over the room as each of us momentarily reflected on the vagaries of life, its unexpected twists, and our assigned roles in the human comedy. Our brief reveries were interrupted by Joanne's bright voice: "I'll make a fresh pot of coffee. Now who wants another piece of pie?"

School Daze

Hank Thompson, a tall young man in his mid-thirties, hurried along the halls of a Midwestern suburban elementary school, thinking about death. He could visualize his tombstone and the date of his demise as October 3, 1985.

Only three weeks on the job and I could die today, Hank thought to himself as he surveyed the main corridor of his school. *This isn't what I expected when I became a principal.*

Everything had changed so suddenly. Ten minutes ago he was in his office speaking to Bob Jameson, the superintendent of schools, who had attended his school's Meet The Teacher Night the previous evening and was calling to congratulate Hank on how well the evening had been organized. The next minute, Harriet, Hank's secretary, was buzzing him on the intercom—something he knew in just the short time of working with her that she would never do when he was speaking to the superintendent unless it was urgent.

"I'm sorry, Bob, but Harriet is buzzing me which means there's some kind of emergency," Hank said quickly.

"No problem," Bob replied and Hank knew that Bob fully understood, for he had been an elementary school principal before moving into central administration posts.

Hank pressed the key to the intercom.

"What's up?" he asked.

Harriet began speaking unusually fast.

"Hank, I just got a call from a parent, Mrs. Bennett, who told me that as she was pulling into our parking lot, she saw a woman in a parking space across from her get out of her car and open the trunk and she pulled out a rifle and walked into the school. Mrs. Bennett immediately called the police and then she called us."

Harriet, renowned for her calm demeanor under the most stressful circumstances, betrayed her heightened concern by the rapid-fire presentation of these facts and a rising pitch to her voice.

For a few seconds Hank sat immobilized, saying nothing, his brain struggling to formulate any plan of action under such dire, unexpected events. Then, in some quixotic trick of the mind, he flashed back to his final interview with the Board of Education, just two months ago, when, in answer to some Board member's question, he had pronounced his view that "a principal must be prepared to demonstrate leadership in all aspects of the community life of an elementary school." With blazing clarity he knew that this was the biggest test of leadership he could possibly face and all that proud talk and all the schooling and all the observations of other school principals in this middle-class Indiana bedroom community didn't prepare him adequately for this challenge. Now it was the welfare—should he dare think the lives?—of four hundred students and forty-two staff members that were in his hands. He knew that Harriet was waiting for some response and that he had to spring into action.

"Don't share this with anyone," he said in a conspiratorial voice, as though the walls of his office had ears. "Who else knows about this?"

"Only Ginny," Harriet said, referring to the clerk in the school's main office, whose desk was just a few feet away from Harriet's.

"We don't want a panic," he cautioned. "Call the custodian and ask him to come to my office immediately. I'll get on the loud speaker."

"Right," she said and hung up.

His plan book contained emergency procedures for fires, severe snow storms and even tornadoes, but nothing, he noted, for some deranged person entering the school with a rifle. He'd have to make up a plan as he went along and time was against him. He picked up the microphone from the shelf next to his desk and flipped the switch on the control panel. He glanced at his watch and saw that the art, music and gym classes would be changing in four minutes and the school's hallways would be crowded with kids and staff. He cleared his throat and spoke into the microphone, intent on keeping his voice calm and natural.

"Please excuse this interruption, but may I have everyone's attention. This is a new drill procedure. Will all students and teachers please remain where you are until further notice? I repeat: all students and teachers remain where you are until further notice. For anyone currently traveling in the halls, please return to your classroom as quickly as possible. Thank you for your cooperation."

Hank clicked the loudspeaker switch off and hurried out to Harriet's desk, just outside his office. He motioned to Ginny, the office clerk, to join him for a quick conference.

"Ginny, I want you to call each classroom on the intercom and tell the teachers to lock the classroom door and pull the shade down on the glass panel in the door. If they ask why, tell them we're trying to locate a suspicious person who was seen entering the building. They should remain calm and keep the kids busy until we issue an all-clear over the loudspeaker."

Ginny nodded and returned to her desk where the intercom panel was located. Gordon, the young custodian, entered the office. Hank quickly told Gordon what was occurring and his plan for the two of them. Gordon, his jaw muscles twitching, said nothing but nodded his agreement. Hank turned back to Harriet.

"Gordon and I are going to search the school. As soon as we leave the office, lock the two doors. When the police arrive, get on the loudspeaker and ask me to return to the office. Nothing else; just that."

Harriet shook her head, then asked, "Hank, what about any kids in the bathrooms when you made your announcement?"

"Damn!" Hank said in frustration, "I forgot about them."

All day long there was a stream of kids leaving their classrooms and heading for the bathrooms. Teachers had a system that only permitted one girl and boy out of the classroom at a time. Hank did a quick mental calculation and felt frustrated when he realized that as many as forty kids could be wandering the halls, finding themselves locked out of their classrooms. Instantly, he formulated another plan.

"Gordon, you take A Wing and any kids you find in the halls, take them to the library and tell the librarian to keep them occupied. I'll take B Wing and bring any kids I find to the gym. Harriet, call the librarian and the gym teacher and tell them to expect us. We'll give five loud knocks as a signal.

"What about the kids outside on the playground having recess?" Harriet asked.

"I'll round them up and their teachers can bring them into the gym from the outside entrance," Hank said quickly, heading out the office door.

"Hank, maybe you should wait for the police," Harriet said, concern clearly marking her face.

"Once we get all the kids into secure areas, we'll return here," Hank said to Gordon, adding another detail to his plan of action.

Both men step out of the office and hear the click of the door lock and the window shade descending behind them. They hurry to the school lobby like soldiers racing forward to a battle, adrenalin rushing, momentarily heedless of personal danger, guided instinctively by duty and responsibility, intent on protecting the safety of four hundred kids. They reach the lobby and wordlessly, with only a mutually fleeting glance, part and head down the hallway of the two main corridors.

Now it's the war zone, Hank thinks, blood pulsing at his temples, his mouth dry, fists clenched. Images of his wife and two kids suddenly flood his brain. *Kissed them goodbye this morning--was that the last time? What about Gordon? He has three kids and another on the way.* Hank's brain is working at the speed of light.

No one in the long corridor—look into cafeteria— what's that noise?—it's coming from the kitchen—race

along cafeteria wall—peek through glass in door—
kitchen ladies, chatting and preparing lunch—maybe
didn't hear announcement—act casual—"Hi, ladies—
possible intruder—lock kitchen doors"—back into
hallway—no signs of anyone—check boys' bathroom—
three boys in stalls—hustle them out—"Follow me!"—
check girls' bathroom—open door and call in, "Anyone
in here?"—little girl's voice, "I'm not finished."—boys
behind me giggling—"Hurry up!"—flushing of toilet—
first-grader appears—"Come with me!"—five loud
knocks on gym door—leave kids with gym teacher—she
looks worried but no time for explanation—reach exit to
playground—swarms of kids, three teachers--quick,
casual instructions—"Please, no questions,"—hustle
everyone into side entrance of gym—gym teacher now
looks like she's about to burst into tears—back into
corridor—feel heart racing—forgot to check teachers'
lunchroom—damn, no glass panel in door—hard to
breathe—lunchroom empty—where the hell is she?—
who the hell is she?—is she after someone or just a
random maniac?—can see the headlines—pounding
headache—please, God, not the kids—shirt sopping
wet—eerily quiet—what was that noise?—click of the
loudspeaker?—"Mr. Thompson, please return to the
office."—Harriet's calm voice—"Mr. Thompson, please
return to the office."—cops must be here—thank God,

but anything could still happen—want to see my sons again--want to tell my wife I love her—want to live!

Hank hurries past the lobby and down the short hallway towards the main office, glancing through the large windows to see four or five police cars parked helter-skelter in front of the school entrance. Policemen are donning flak jackets and taking rifles and other gear out of their car trunks.

Harriet is peeping from behind the closed shade on the door to the office and opens the door at Hank's approach. Hank immediately sees Police Chief Redman.

"You should have waited for us," the chief says sternly, but before Hank can answer, Redman continues; "Anything new to report?"

"No," replies Hank, surprised to find he's still breathing hard.

"Any known visitors in the building?"

"We haven't checked on that yet," Hank says sheepishly, because that thought hadn't entered his mind.

"Let's do that!" the chief says brusquely.

"I'll take care of it," Harriet offers and heads for the public address microphone at her desk. In a calm voice she broadcasts her message: "Attention, all teachers. Please report any visitors currently in your classrooms. Please call the office immediately with this information. Thank you."

Just then Hank realizes that a few classrooms and the library face the front entrance and can see the police cars and the officers with the rifles. *The kids will freak out,* he thinks. *And probably the teachers, too.*

Sweat is pouring into his eyes, making it hard for him to see the chief. Before he can share his concern, the chief says abruptly, "You stay put. We'll take it from here," and quickly exits the office. Hank goes into his private office from where he can see the police quietly entering the building. Then, in one jarring crescendo, the ringing phones in the main office and the buzzing from the intercom interrupt all thoughts. A minute later Harriet appears at his door and in a calm voice says: "Mrs. Harrison from across the street saw the police cars arriving and wants to know what's happening. And the superintendent is on line two asking for an update on the emergency. And the librarian is on the intercom, hysterical—she saw the police cars."

His mind racing with thoughts on how to handle these new challenges, Hank still hears the intercom buzzing in the background. Ginny appears behind Harriet at the door of Hank's office and is clearly excited.

"Mr. Thompson, Mr. Thompson," Ginny calls in a loud voice as though he were far away and both Harriet and Hank stare expectantly at her. "I think we found the lady with the rifle."

Hank's pulse quickens again, this time to a beat that he thinks must surely cause some blood vessel to burst.

"You won't believe this!" Ginny exclaims, adding a note of puzzlement to the unbearable tension. She breaks into a smile and Hank can't stand it an instant longer and bursts forth with a loud, irritable "What?"

Ginny enters his office and positions herself between Hank and Harriet. She pauses for what seems like an eternity, clearly enjoying her moment in the spotlight. Hank's nerves are screaming and he thinks of slapping her.

"Monica Jeffries—she's the substitute teacher that we got at the last minute this morning when Mary Welch called in sick," Ginny says, referring to an absent first-grade teacher. "She just called to say that a mother was in her room who had come to deliver an heirloom musket that her son wanted to share with his classmates for Show and Tell, and now the mother wants to leave."

Harriet interjects quickly, "Monica hasn't been a substitute in our building before and she wouldn't know your new policy about having all visitors report to the office first."

"But it's listed on the general rules that every substitute teacher is supposed to read!" Hank shouts, angry frustration masking the deeper relief springing up inside him. With this small explosion, he releases all the pent-up anxiety and fear and maddening thoughts he's been struggling with for the last—how long has it actually been?—twenty minutes. He can feel his heartbeat subsiding to a more normal rhythm as tension slowly oozes out of his body.

"I guess our crisis is over," he says, forcing a small smile in Harriet and Ginny's direction. "We'll certainly learn from this, although, thank God, it was a false alarm. Harriet, let's put a new emergency procedure for intruders on the agenda for the next faculty meeting. Call it Code Red. Ginny, get on the loudspeaker and ask the chief to return to the office immediately. I'll announce an All Clear as soon as I speak to the chief."

Hank glances at his phone and sees the blinking light on line two.

'I'll take the call from the superintendent now."

The two women hasten to carry out Hank's instructions as he reaches for the phone. *After this is over*, he thinks, *I want to call my wife.* He feels an urgent need to hear her voice, with the kids laughing and playing in the background. He glances at her picture on his desk, her arms around their two young boys, and a surge of love courses through him. To his great surprise, tears are welling up at the corners of his eyes. He wipes his eyes with his hands and speaks into the phone.

"We had a few minutes of high tension here, Bob, but it's over now and we're back to normal."

He hears the superintendent chuckling and he knows that Bob will enjoy this story which, in his own mind, is already taking on the dimensions of myth, to be told and retold through future years as a dramatic farce, inviting embellishments and humorous asides. Than he notices that his hand holding the phone is shaking uncontrollably.

The 6:10 to Chappaqua

All his thoughts were about love.

How do you fall out of love? Does it take place over a long stretch of time, as, incrementally, petty annoyances, minor disagreements, suppressed resentments, casual indifference and harbored slights accrue to some finite moment when, Eureka!, the light bulb clicks on and you wake up one morning and there it is, this cold, hard fact, staring you down? This person who was once the center of your universe and sharer of your dreams, and with whom you've now spent x number of years, shared your body and revealed your soul, no longer occupies your heart. This person is now merely someone moving innocuously in tandem with you through each day's set routine, unnoticed and unloved.

Or is it something organic: the natural evolution of personalities growing and changing through the years until two different people emerge, as though from a chrysalis, and are suddenly surprised to find themselves shackled to a stranger?

Such dire thoughts were occupying David Atwater's mind as he rode the commuter train home from his Manhattan office. The New York Times was propped open in front of him, but he was not reading it. More importantly, he thought, how does a new love glide unexpectedly into the slipstream of your life, awakening long dormant curiosities, giddy feelings and heady desires resulting in a rush of dissatisfaction with your status quo?

Any other passenger observing the furrowed brow and twitching jaw muscles on the handsome, rugged-featured, forty-nine-year-old face of the tall, well-dressed man, might have assumed that he was responding to some newspaper article that aroused his interest or concern. But David Atwater was lost in a welter of thoughts and mounting anxiety.

He had to get his thoughts straight. Clear his mind. Create talking points as he did when addressing his company's board members. Clear explanations—he owed Susan that much. But, Jesus, there were no clear explanations.

What words could he use to convey his jumbled feelings? *Thanks for the twenty-six years of married life we've shared and the two fine kids we raised and successfully guided into adulthood? Thanks for your loyalty and support when I was rising through the corporate ranks and fighting turf wars and missing from home a lot, shifting the family burdens mostly to you? Thanks for keeping yourself slim and attractive and managing an orderly home and being a gracious hostess? But somewhere along the way we lost each other—those little shared moments of intimacy—I'm not talking about sex although that certainly became mechanical after a while—but those elliptical gestures or spontaneous, private laughs or the sudden flush of mutual excitement about some future plans, or nuanced eye contact that made us feel we occupied a special, private, bonded world.*

You've always been analytic rather than emotional. While I'm super analytic in my work, maybe I'm too emotional in my private life—a hard thing to admit for a man—but for any problems we've faced during the years, in trying to resolve our differences, you've always left me with the feeling that you would calculate the pro's and con's of each side and arrive at some conclusion based on a rational analysis. That's the way you decide everything, including, you said, choosing me as your husband over Billy Barrett who also proposed to you. You decide the deeply personal issues in our relationship the way you decide on a new dining room table or what college was best suited for our daughter or what dentist to go to.

No, he objected, that makes me sound like I've been storing everything up like some squirrel with its nuts and now I'm throwing it all at her in one barrage. Besides, he admitted, they all sound like excuses to justify a selfish urge to be with someone else. But that urge is so strong! Overwhelming, really.

He had always been proud of her, but now he thought how pride was, in a sense, an objectifying emotion—proud of his son's college record, proud of his wife's youthful figure, proud of his golf game—something that becomes static, distancing, like a trophy for some past achievement resting permanently in a display case, removed from any current, emotional association but mentioned in passing on suitable occasions.

He decided that he couldn't and wouldn't give Susan any reasons. It was what it was and that was all there was to it. He didn't want to hurt her—as if that could be avoided—he just wanted out. What country was it where the man simply said, 'I divorce you," and the matter was settled? Obviously, some third-world country where the men had all the rights. When she got over her shock, Susan would probably want a big settlement. Even though she inherited all that money from her mother, demanding big bucks to compensate for being discarded was the pound of flesh that most women insisted on. Okay, he'd give her anything she wanted—within reason—just to be free.

Of course she would want to know who the other woman was. That would be a shocker! Catherine and

Steve Maxwell had been their closest friends for how long? Our kids were little when they moved to Chappaqua and we met them at the club. He liked both of them tremendously from the start. They had been transplanted from Colorado when Steve got a big promotion to his company's corporate headquarters in New York City, and they had none of that taut-lipped, vulpine, sharp-eyed sophisticated veneer that marked so many of the up-and-coming people he and Susan interacted with.

Steve, an accounting wizard, was portly and jolly and a great golfing partner, not only for his masterful game but for his robust humor and appealing personality. He had the gift of making other men—even the most competitive men—feel relaxed and congenial in his presence.

Catherine seemed the perfect match for Steve: as open as the Western skies and totally unaffected. Mother of three, she had been a nurse before meeting Steve in a hospital where he was having his appendix removed. As she told the story in a charming, self-deprecating way, it was love at first slice. Catherine was pretty with an even-featured, good-complexioned, fresh-scrubbed look. Her body, soft and curvaceous, defied the current trend for super thin and angular. Her curly copper hair was arranged in no particular style—just a short, casual bob that framed her face attractively.

Catherine was the most thoughtful person, remembering birthdays and anniversaries and sending get-well cards when his kids were sick. The Maxwell home was modest, by Chappaqua standards, furnished in a utilitarian style to accommodate three rambunctious kids—now all grown like his—and their entertainment was refreshingly simple. Catherine cooked meals that reminded him of his childhood: mostly roasts and mashed potatoes and vegetables and home-made cakes and pies; nothing that was faddy or had a foreign name. It was her welcoming spirit and infectious gaiety that made evenings at the Maxwell home so special.

He remembered how Susan, much more reserved and self-aware, did not warm to Catherine at first. Only when she decided that Catherine's enthusiasm and earthiness were guileless did she finally accept her and ultimately embrace her as a friend.

From the beginning he liked everything about Catherine, especially her honesty and warmth and the way she cocked her head while her big blue eyes locked on yours as she listened to some story you were telling her. She had a broad encouraging smile, and she actually giggled—a distinctive trait that set her apart from all the women in their set.

A lot of people at the club dismissed Catherine and Steve as hickish, but David immediately—and Susan ultimately—forged a strong, intimate bond with them.

David knew from the start that he was physically attractive to Catherine's cushiony voluptuousness but, adhering to the social code of his class and in deference to his friendship with Steve, he locked these thoughts in the back of his mind, only to find them escaping when he'd glimpse her in a bathing suit at the club's pool or watch her on the dance floor in some gown that accentuated her lushness.

Catherine's uninhibited and instinctively honest remarks to him—compliments on his fitness, his clothes, his natural grace and sophisticated manner—could have been misconstrued as flirtatious except that they lacked any self-conscious or lascivious overtones. Catherine was, *sui generis,* Catherine, he thought.

The friendship between the two couples blossomed. Soon, vacations with all five kids were being planned as well as weekend excursions to sites in the New England states that Catherine and Steve had never seen and that David and Susan enjoyed showing them.

"Aren't they a wonderful couple!" was David's oft-repeated comment to Susan at the conclusion of some excursion. "So refreshing in their enthusiasm for everything!"

Susan would give him a thin smile and murmur her assent.

For over ten years their strong friendship had flourished until it was a set piece in their lives and taken for granted. Then, just three months ago, at Christmas time, Susan and David were giving their annual holiday dinner party and, of course, Catherine and Steve headed the guest list. Catherine arrived without Steve, saying he had come down with a bad cold.

"But I didn't want to miss your wonderful party, so here I am!" she said in her usual ebullient style, her eyes dancing with excitement and her wide smile radiating joy and warmth. She looked exceptionally pretty tonight, he thought.

It had begun to snow shortly before the first guests had arrived, lightly at first but then heavily through the evening. David, ever mindful of his duties as a host, had seen that everyone's wine glasses at dinner were refilled, and cognac and liqueurs were passed around the table after dessert. He noticed that Catherine drank more than usual and grew more animated throughout the evening. By the time the guests were leaving, he was concerned. He was helping Catherine on with her coat when she turned to him and said, "David, I'm not a good driver in snow. Would you mind taking me home?"

Susan, standing by the open front door, as wind gusts blew snow into the foyer, said quickly, "Of course he will," in that decisive tone that brooked no opposition. David was fleetingly annoyed that Susan had made the generous gesture that he wanted to make, but he just smiled and said, "Sure."

Driving carefully in the mounting snow, the ride took twenty minutes and passed mostly in uncharacteristic silence, as Catherine seemed in an unusually subdued mood and David was focusing on the tricky road conditions. Finally, he pulled into her circular driveway and stopped in front of her door.

Catherine looked up at the second floor of her house. "Steve must be asleep," she said quietly. He started to open his door to walk around and open the passenger door, but her hand caught his arm. "Could we talk for a minute?" she asked in a voice so deep and serious that he was momentarily jarred. He shut his door and turned his face to her. Then he saw the tears on her cheeks and was more confused.

Looking straight ahead, Catherine spoke in a hushed voice, her words coming haltingly.

"I think you should know that I've decided to leave Steve."

He heard this news with total disbelief. An awkward silence followed, and he realized she was waiting for his response.

"What can I say?" he finally said, feeling utterly stupid. "I'm flabbergasted!"

Catherine looked down at her folded hands on her lap and then gave him a quick sidelong glance.

"Do you want to know why I'm leaving him?" she asked, and he thought he detected a surprisingly sly edge in her tone.

"Only if you care to tell me," was all he could muster.

"Because I've fallen in love with another man," she said, staring out through the window at the enveloping snow, tears still glistening on her cheeks.

Marriage breakups were common in his set, especially after the children were grown and two people, left alone, were forced to confront everything that seemed missing from the current state of their relationship. At that stage, susceptibility to the allure of others was rampant.

"These things happen," he said, hoping to be supportive, but his mind was racing, trying to come up with who the man might be.

As if she were reading his thoughts, Catherine said, "Don't you want to know the man?"

"I'm certainly curious," he admitted.

Her head swiveled quickly and her eyes, shiny with tears, stared directly into his.

"You!" she said, before turning away and staring down at her hands again. Now her words came rapidly. "I'm sorry, David. I've tried to fight these feelings for a long time but I can't any longer. Steve is a wonderful guy but there's nothing left between us—no affection, hardly any sex—and then every time I'm with you, I feel happy and alive and even young again."

She paused and shot him a half-smile. "You're quite the charmer, you know. All the women are attracted to you."

He sat there like a statue, the muscles in his face frozen in a perpetual look of muddled surprise. Catherine turned her head away and began sobbing. "I know it's hopeless. I know you're happily married and I don't want to hurt anybody, but I can't deny my feelings any longer." She paused, as if weighing her next words. "I've decided to go back to Colorado and start a new life." Her voice rose to almost a scream. "Oh, god, I shouldn't have told you. I'm so ashamed. Forgive me."

She turned suddenly and leaned her face into his shoulder, her body shaking with each sob. Instinctively, he pulled her toward him, wrapping his arms around her and giving her back comforting pats. Then he became aware of the fresh scent of her hair and the aroma of a delicate perfume she was wearing and the soft, inviting flesh his arms were encircling, and his shock and confusion slipped away, pushed out by sheer desire.

Catherine's hand rose up and caressed his cheek. She raised her face from his chest and looked up at him. "Can you forgive me, David?" she said quietly.

He gazed down at her soft, tearful eyes, her wet cheeks and her moist lips, half parted, and for a moment he thought he was watching some trite, romantic movie and the camera was zooming in on the star for her close-up. Then he realized that he was part of this scene and, acting solely on primeval impulse, he rushed toward those beckoning lips, devouring them with his own.

Her breath was fresh and minty, which surprised him when he thought of the food and liquor she had consumed. His tongue shot past her teeth as his arms tightened around her yielding shoulders. She arched her body so that her large, soft breasts were pushing against his chest, and her hands now clutched the back of his head tightly. He was fully aroused, mindless of everything except this desirable women in his arms and the urge to explore every inch of her body.

Their fevered necking continued until abruptly she pulled away and leaned against the passenger door. Confusion again swept over him.

"This is crazy!" We can't...I'm sorry," she said in staccato fashion.

Before he could make any reply, she had opened the car door and was rushing up the walk. He watched her disappear inside the house and sat motionless in his car, stunned by what had just taken place.

When he finally drove home, the house was dark. He undressed and slipped quietly into bed beside his sleeping wife, but his mind continued to race with fleeting images and conflicted thoughts. Sleep refused to come.

What startled him the most was the feeling that a door had suddenly, unexpectedly been opened to him, through which he glimpsed a thrilling new world of exciting possibilities. But this new vista had just as suddenly caused him to look back on the world he currently inhabited with new scrutiny.

As he listened to his wife's even breathing and felt the vibration when her limbs occasionally twitched, he asked himself daring questions that resulted in troubling answers, jolting him into the realization that although he was a contented man, he was not a happy one. Not truly happy!

His work was demanding and rewarding, especially financially, but he had lost the lust for battle, the insatiable thirst for more: more competitive victories, more money, more glory. His two children, Rachel and Craig, were grown, launched on successful careers and neither was yet married. They lived separate lives, returning home for holidays and occasional weekend visits. At these times he was proud of the adults they had become, yet he recognized that the very independence he and Susan had fostered in them was now culminating in their treating their parents as equals, inhibiting any child-parent intimacy that he had always enjoyed.

His focus turned to Susan and an emotional numbness set in. Yes, he felt gratitude and respect for his wife and enjoyed the comfortableness of their regulated life together. With the children gone, they had quietly settled into a well-defined pattern of daily life that, when examined, revealed the tedium at its core. From deep recesses of his mind crept forth a litany of unresolved minor grievances and petty imperfections that, cumulatively, left him feeling unsettled and rueful.

He forced himself to turn away from these dark, dangerous thoughts, taking flights of fancy about what life with Catherine might be like. Catherine the effervescent; Catherine the sensitive; Catherine the voluptuary.

Strong sensual images crowded his brain as he finally drifted off to sleep.

The next day at his office he got a call from Catherine. Still befuddled by his warring feelings but curious to hear what she might say now in the cold-sober day, he took the call.

"David, I know you must be very busy but I had to call you," she said in a breathy voice, her words rushing out. "I must apologize for my behavior last night. I'm afraid I had too much to drink at your party. I should never have burdened you with my problems." A short pause, filled with loud silence. "Can you forgive me?"

Smitten with her delicious voice, he said, too brightly, "There's nothing to forgive."

Her tone registered a lower pitch. "Yes there is. My leaving Steve and my feelings for you are two separate issues. I know you and Susan have a great relationship. I would never want to hurt her. I should never have told you the way I felt."

He held the phone closer to his mouth and in a low, intimate voice said, "I'm glad you did."

"Please don't be cruel, David. Don't mock my feelings," she said, self-pity surrounding her words.

He responded quickly. "Catherine, I'm not mocking you. I'm trying to say that I return your feelings."

"You mean you love me?" came the explosive, probing response.

All his conflictive ruminations, endless questions and pleasurable fantasies of the past twelve hours were now condensed as he was confronted with a simple question, subtracting him to a point, pinioning him with its directness. The word *love* echoed in his brain like an incessant drumbeat reverberating through his senses, sending him reeling with indecision.

"Do you?" Catherine asked with imposing impatience and rising excitement in her tone that overwhelmed his chaotic and cautionary voices, forcing him to make an unexpectedly definitive declaration. His vanity was suddenly unbridled, and, in a burst of recaptured youthful exuberance, he found himself committed to saying, "I do."

Catherine's reply came in a rush. "Oh, David, I never dreamed...that is, I only hoped...oh, darling, this is wonderful!"

He was grinning like a kid at the circus. How long had it been since anyone had called him *darling*?

Catherine rushed on. "David, we have to talk. When can we meet? I could come to Manhattan tomorrow."

Still grinning he glanced at his appointment schedule for the next day and saw that if he postponed a meeting with the company treasurer, his afternoon could be free.

"The afternoon looks good," he said. "After one. Where would you like to meet for lunch?"

Her answer came after a short pause.

"We can't meet in public. It's too dangerous. Can we get a room?"

He was hoping she'd say that as he didn't want to appear to be rushing things. With mounting excitement, he heard Catherine say, "Get a room, darling (again that thrilling use of *darling*) under the name of Mr. and Mrs. Dawson and I'll meet you in the room. Just tell me which hotel."

"The St. Regis," he said without hesitating, avoiding the hotels where his company put up out-of-town guests and had rooms on reserve. "One thirty."

"Remember, Mr. and Mrs. Dawson, D...A...W...S...O...N."

"Yes, okay."

"One-thirty," she repeated. "I'll be there. Goodbye, darling."

He heard the click on the other end and sat in silence, still cradling the phone to his ear. He couldn't quite believe everything that had taken place in the last few minutes: his declaration of love; the assignation that had been quickly set up; Catherine's impetuousness; her cleverness. He hadn't felt like this since he had asked the prettiest girl in his class to his high school senior prom and she'd said yes.

His thoughts suddenly shifted to Susan with a tinge of guilt, but somehow she seemed obscurely distant, removed from this new-found excitement in his life, and his thoughts quickly shifted back to Catherine and visions of tomorrow. He was crossing the Rubicon and heading down an uncharted path to a destination yet unknown, but it was such a heady, pulse-quickening adventure that he was heedlessly eager for it. Impulse and desire were overruling his rational side as he mindlessly followed this unexpected turn in his life. Blind to where this caprice could take him, he was giddy with expectations and gave no thought to anything but tomorrow afternoon.

* * * *

The next three months passed in a whirl of secret meetings, passionate couplings, shared intimacies and exhilarating subterfuge. Catherine was adroit at creating excuses for visits to Manhattan, besides shopping forays, and he, in turn, created plausible scenarios for his being absent from the office in the afternoon.

Everything with Catherine seemed new and exciting. He found himself laughing more—even giggling—with her. Like some drunken sailor on a weekend bender, he was besotted with her: her body; her uninhibited sexual inventiveness; her openness and warmth; her constant demonstrations of affection and professed interest in everything he was interested in. He loved the way she'd lay with her head resting on his shoulder after prolonged, frenetic lovemaking, her head tilted up and her eyes gazing intently at him, as he told her details of his life and dreams.

With her eager guidance and hints of departing soon for Colorado and making a formal brake with Steve, he came to the decision that he couldn't live without her and then was determined to jettison his present life for a permanent one with her, regardless of the cost. He was convinced that she was the key to any future happiness he might enjoy in his advancing middle years.

He could afford to take an early retirement, and they talked about starting anew in Colorado. The prospect of exciting adventures, the nascent thrill of starting over, recapturing the dormant spirit of his youth and eagerly charting a new life course, filled his fantasies and fueled his headlong rush toward startling decisions. Fixated on a thrilling future, his present humdrum life was quickly receding into the past. Just one troubling detail remained: Susan.

* * * *

"Next stop Chappaqua," booms the conductor, interrupting his thoughts. He folds the *Times* and places it in his briefcase before leaving his seat and walking to the door, his mind now focusing on the scene to be played out with Susan—a scene he is not looking forward to but is resolved to initiate.

In earnest concentration, he drives the short distance from the Chappaqua station to his home. On entering the house, he's greeted by Baxter and Clutch, their two Airedales—he loves dogs and so does Catherine, but Susan only tolerates them and keeps her distance—and gets a cheery hello from Stella, their full-time housekeeper, who is setting the table for dinner. Susan insisted on a formal, sit-down dinner in the dining room each night with just the two of them, he thinks irritably.

Occasionally, she'd relent and let him change into casual clothes and they'd eat in the family room while watching the news on television. Tonight he welcomes the formal setting as a distancing device for what he is about to announce.

He walks to the family room and makes his ritual homecoming Bombay martini. Susan, in the adjoining kitchen, gives him an abstract wave and a small-voiced "Hi," before crossing the short distance to join him at the bar. When did they stop kissing hello, he wonders, comparing this cold, empty greeting with the passionate kisses and abundant hugs that Catherine gives him.

"Dinner will be ready in a half-hour," Susan announces with all the efficiency of the railroad conductor who announced the next stop was Chappaqua: sharp, precise and sticking to the schedule.

"Oh, by the way," she says in that flat voice that was all business, "Catherine called. She wanted you to call her as soon as you got home. Something about a surprise gift for Steve's birthday next week—a golf club or something. She sounded urgent, but why such a fuss over a birthday present I don't understand."

His antennae are instantly up, listening for any hint of suspicion or awareness in her voice, but he hears nothing. Still, his senses jump to full alert and he can feel his whole body tensing.

"Might as well call her now," he says, trying to sound casual as he takes his drink and walks to the phone in the kitchen. He doesn't want to use his cell phone where he has her number on speed dial.

"She's not home," Susan says, still in a flat monotone. "She left her cell number. It's on the counter"

He knows her cell number from memory but picks up the piece of paper from the counter and pretends to be reading it as he dials. Susan is standing behind the bar, pouring herself a diet soda; she never drinks at home, fearful of gaining weight. The phone rings three times before he hears Catherine's urgent "Hello."

"Hi, Catherine. It's David," he says with forced cheerfulness in too loud a voice, trying to sound casual. "Susan tells me you want my advice on a golf club for Steve. How can I help you?" He smiles at Susan who is only a short distance away, leafing through a fashion magazine—one of many she subscribes to.

Catherine's voice is low and harsh. "David, I'm sorry, but I can't go through with it. I'll call you tomorrow at the office to explain." Then her voice shifts to a softer tone. "Please forgive me," and he hears the click on the other end.

He keeps the phone to his ear, paralyzed with confusion. A five-second phone monologue has just altered the course of his life, like a doctor telling him that he had some incurable disease. Hurt and anger and wounded pride and puzzlement grab him by the throat and he can barely breathe. Frozen in silence, he stares out the kitchen window, grappling with his onrush of conflicting feelings. Then he hears his wife's voice, and he realizes she's now standing next to him.

"What's the matter?" she asks,

Momentarily his focus returns to her and he has the presence of mind to say, "Oh, she had another call. She'll call back." He puts the phone down.

"You're as white as a sheet," she says. "Are you feeling alright?"

"What? Oh, yes," he answers distractedly, trying frantically to collect his thoughts. He drains his martini in one giant gulp, as his wife's face registers surprise, and he heads toward the bar, keeping his back to her. From across the room he hears her voice droning on about a dinner party at the Henderson's after the charity golf tournament this coming Saturday, but her voice is fading in and out, and his mind is careening like a pin-ball machine.

What happened? How could Catherine do this to him? All their plans for an exciting new life—dashed. How cruel! How fucking cruel! Had he misjudged her completely? Was she only toying with him? All his questions and speculations are pummeling his ego. Indignation and rage are quickly overtaking him. Again,

Susan's voice drifts into his consciousness, this time much nearer. "David, you're shaking," she says, touching his arm, a clear note of concern now present in her voice. "Are you ill?"

His mind flips back to the present. "No, just a little lightheaded," he says, trying for a casual tone. "A rough day," he adds by way of a feeble explanation for his present distracted state. "I think I'll lie down for a bit."

"Shall I call you when dinner's ready?" she asks, ever practical and efficient.

"Yes," he answers, striding briskly out of the room and hurrying up the stairs to their bedroom, where he heads straight for the bathroom and rinses his face in cold water, hoping to clear his mind, to make sense of what has just happened, to extract order from the onslaught of chaos. He raises his head, droplets of water still caught in his eyebrows and ambling down his cheeks.

He stares at his reflection in the mirror but doesn't see himself. His eyes are searching for the familiar features and contours, but his mind has taken total control, and the image that's visible is not the one appearing in the mirror but a strange visage, devoid of any personal characteristics, laughing at him. Laughing at him for his foolishness, his stupidity, his adolescent romanticism, his reckless desire to feel special again. The laughing, sneering face mocks him, calls him a whinny, middle-aged, never-satisfied malcontent.

Slowly the mocking image dissolves into his own reflection and he examines his face as if seeing it for the first time: graying at the temples; rumpled with deepening crevices; a disdainful curl to the lip; incipient jowls; thinning hairline.

He hears Susan calling from the bedroom, "David?" Reaching for a towel, he dries his face. "I'm in here," he says quietly.

"I just came to see how you are," she says, and he unexpectedly finds comfort in her voice.

"I'll be fine," he says, returning to the bedroom. "I just need a little time."

"Yes, of course," she says, turning down the coverlet on their bed and plumping the pillows. Now she turns to him and there's a small smile circling the corners of her mouth. Her gaze is calm and steady. "You take all the time you need. I'll wait for you. We can have dinner in the family room and watch the news. When you're ready."

He watches her as she walks toward the bedroom door, a slim, graceful figure. She turns and cocks her head. "If Catherine calls back, I'll take care of it. Just relax. Everything will be fine."

Her smile has widened, and it's the last thing he sees before plunging head-first into the familiar, soothing comfort of their bed.

The Surprise

At 11AM the data processing offices on the top floor of New York City's famous Macy's Department Store were humming with activity. Maureen Peterson was routinely entering figures on her computer when the door to the Accounts Receivable office opened and the boy appeared. He stood just inside the door surveying the occupants, six females in all, before approaching Maureen.

She didn't notice him until he was standing next to her desk and said, "Excuse me, ma'am." Annoyed by this unexpected interruption, Maureen looked away from her computer screen and beheld a child of extraordinary beauty. He was small, appearing to be no more than seven or eight, with a narrow, delicate frame. The contours of his face were sharply etched with a firm, dimpled chin, high, pronounced cheekbones and a dazzling coloration of very fair skin set off by curly black hair, black brows and lashes and the most vivid green eyes Maureen had ever seen. So taken was she by this startling apparition that she stared in mute appreciation for many seconds before responding, and in that brief time she had a vague sense that, as young as he was, he had an easy understanding of the effect his appearance had on people.

He was dressed neatly in a white short-sleeve shirt and tan slacks suitable for the early summer weather they were experiencing in May. He shifted from one foot to the other and offered her a tentative smile, revealing white, even teeth.

"I'm sorry to bother you," he said, as if sensing Maureen's momentary annoyance at being interrupted, "but could I please use your phone? It's an emergency."

With these last words his entire demeanor changed: his emerald green eyes clouded over and his mouth turned down at the corners. He looked as if he was about to cry.

Only in her mid-twenties and single, Maureen's maternal instincts were nevertheless instantly aroused by this beautiful child and his tremulous expression.

"What's the matter?" she asked, her voice full of kind solicitude, giving him her whole attention. He was standing a few feet away from her desk but now he moved to her side and in a soft, confidential voice, intended only for her, spoke haltingly.

"I need to call the police," he said and seemed more distraught with each word he uttered.

Alarmed, Maureen asked, "Why do you want to call the police?"

The boy's beautiful face was now crinkled with concern, as his furrowed brows sunk into his eyes and his chin trembled as he spoke. The words tumbled out in one, long rushing stream.

"I've lost all my money. It was right here in my back pants pocket and then when I went to pay for my brother's surprise birthday present, it was gone, and I don't know what happened to it, but I haven't got any money to get back home and my mother told me if I was ever unsure of what to do, to ask a policeman, and the sales lady at the toy department sent me up here so I could call the police."

The boy looked away as though ashamed to have her see his struggling not to cry. Looking off into the distance, his voice dropped to a whisper as though reflecting on his situation. "My mother's going to be mad and my little brother will be really disappointed. I promised him a surprise for his birthday. He's only six and a baseball mitt is the one thing he wants more than anything in the world." His voice trailed off and his head hung forward in dejection.

Maureen rose from her desk and placed her hands on his shoulders, gently massaging his thin frame.

"There, there, now," she said softly. "Don't be upset. We can work this out. Why don't we call your father?"

She felt his body grow rigid and then he twisted out of her grasp and moved a few steps away.

"I don't have a father!" he said in an angry tone, laced with shame. "He left us two years ago."

Maureen grappled with this new revelation, her good heart brimming with pity and resolve. "Then why don't I call your mother and I'll explain what happened and I'm sure she'll understand."

The boy turned quickly and looked directly at her, his face contorted with anguish.

"You can't call my mother," he said vehemently, then paused, as if collecting his thoughts before continuing. "My mom's in bed. She's very sick and she sleeps a lot. And she'd be mad if she knew I left my little brother in the apartment while she was napping and took the subway here and was spending everything I've saved over the last year to buy him a baseball mitt as a surprise."

Maureen heard all of this though a mist of rising emotions. She pictured a lonely, ailing woman, defeated by the desertion of a husband and the weight of caring for her children alone, and this child trying to fill the shoes of a man and bring his little brother a wonderful birthday surprise. He probably had his pocket picked, she thought, with mounting indignation. Every day the store detectives were arresting pickpockets. They had no shame: now they were stealing from children. She was determined to help this sad, beautiful child and suddenly saw herself as a heroine, bounteously coming to his rescue.

"How much was the baseball mitt?" she asked, hoping to distract him from dwelling any further on his unfortunate family circumstances while she formulated a plan.

"It was twenty-seven dollars with the tax; it's only a junior mitt," he said in a forlorn whisper. "I had $30 with me so I could still get some wrapping paper and have money for the subway home.

"Why don't you go over there and have a seat for a minute," she suggested, gently turning him in the direction of the small bench next to the office door. Something in her voice seemed to reassure him and he followed her instruction, sitting with his shoulders slumped and his head down, the overhead lights casting glimmering shadows on his curly black hair. His entire body conveyed an eloquent expression of youthful despair.

Maureen moved quickly among the desks of her five co-workers, bending low to whisper in each woman's ear, nodding toward the beautiful boy sitting so dejectedly by the door. Each woman would turn to look briefly at the dispirited child, utter some small commiserative exclamation, then remove a bag from a desk drawer and hand money to Maureen. Her mission completed in a matter of minutes, Maureen returned to her desk where she, too, extracted her wallet from her handbag and withdrew a ten-dollar bill. With a triumphant smile on her face, she approached the little figure. He seemed lost in bewildered dejection.

"Here!" she said in a soothing, confident voice, thrusting her hands directly in front of the boy's lowered head and waving a fanned-out display of money at him. "Here's thirty-five dollars: enough for you to buy the mitt for your brother, get some wrapping paper and a nice card and get back home and still have a little extra for yourself to buy some ice cream or candy. So cheer up now; everything's going to be fine."

The boy raised his head to the level of her outstretched hand and gazed intently at the money. His body seemed to grow bigger as he squared his shoulders and then he raised his head to look directly at Maureen and she saw a mixture of relief and happiness registering simultaneously in his green eyes and hesitant smile--a smile that rapidly spread across his face and dazzled Maureen with its electrifying beauty. But the smile vanished quickly, replaced by a wistful look of compunction.

"But I can't take your money. I could never pay you back, except in years," he said, glancing again at the bills.

"It's not a loan. It's a gift from all of us to you," she said triumphantly, thrusting the money into his small hand.

He looked down at the crumpled bills and then, again, gazed into her eyes with such startling intensity that she was mesmerized, feeling like she was being assessed and admired by a grown man. The spell was only momentary and then he erupted from the sofa and, in the totally uninhibited way of the young, threw his arms around her waist, hugging her tightly while his feet danced.

"Oh, thank you. Thank you. Thank you so much. My brother will be so happy. It will be the best surprise he's ever had."

Releasing her, he spoke rapidly. "I should hurry and maybe I can get back before my mom wakes up from her nap. I'll go get the mitt right away."

"Yes, you do that," she said, very pleased with herself, pushing him toward the office door.

She watched his small body almost skip through the door and rush confidently toward the elevator. She stood staring at the back of his head, with that beautiful curly black hair caressing the nape of his neck, and pictured him as a handsome adult. *He'll be a heartbreaker*, she thought. *Such beautiful manners! And so thoughtful!* She could still see his piercing eyes calmly gazing at her when she first noticed him. She felt exultant and surprisingly lighthearted. Another typical dreary day of office routine had suddenly taken an unexpected turn and she had jumped into the moment, playing her part in the unexpected drama with ingenuity and gusto. She had saved the day!

As she returned to her desk, a sly smile streaking across her face, she realized that she didn't even know the boy's name, hadn't even asked, so instantly had she been captivated by his presence and immersed in his sadness. Feeling almost giddy, she decided she'd give him a name: Bobby. Beautiful, sad, fascinating little Bobby. She would long remember him, her Bobby.

Back at her desk, she glanced at her watch. It was almost time for lunch. As always, she was meeting her best friend, Felicia, who had graduated from the same computer school with her and now worked at another department store just a block away.

Maureen was flushed with excitement as she hurried toward the small table in their favorite luncheonette where Felicia was waiting for her. She was barely seated before she burst out with news of her special morning experience. But even as her words tumbled forth in high animation, she took note of the strange expression on Felicia's face. She was just at the point of describing how she had glanced up to see who was interrupting her work when Felicia reached across the table and grabbed her arm with such force that Maureen stopped in mid-sentence.

Felicia spoke quickly. "Curly black hair. Big green eyes. Lost his money for his little brother's surprise birthday present."

"Yes, but how did you know?" Maureen asked, totally confused.

"He was in my office less than a half hour ago," Felicia explained. "We gave him money." Her voice trailed off.

Both women stared mutely into space, grappling with the mysteries of the human heart.

Time Out

The tall, well-dressed man, appearing to be in his early forties, enters the Tap Room of the Royalton Hotel and walks toward the bar.. It's a quiet time in the daily ebb and flow of people: after the cocktail hour and before the theaters and concert halls disgorge their customers. The man quickly surveys the few couples in distant booths and the two men talking intently at one end of the bar, and then heads for a stool at the opposite end. The bartender, young and muscular beneath a starched white shirt and black bow tie, interrupts his housekeeping chores and comes forward, offering a smile and "Good evening."

"Scotch on the rocks," the man says and the drink is quickly delivered. The bartender knows this hotel's protocol: Be polite but don't engage customers in conversation unless initiated by them and keep your comments to a minimum. This customer says nothing beyond "Thanks," when the drink is placed before him, so the bartender retreats to the center of the long, curving bar and resumes arranging liquor bottles.

A few minutes later, an attractive woman, equally well dressed and looking mid-thirties, enters. She stops in front of the bar and her eyes flicker across the well-dressed man before choosing a seat. It's four stools away from his but, because of the curve of the bar, offers the possibility of direct eye contact. The man notices the bartender eyeing her appreciatively. *She's no kid but still she can turn eyes,* the man thinks, and a twitch of excitement passes across his face at the mere prospect of possibilities. Universal man, ever on the hunt!

"Bombay martini, up, rocks on the side, double olive," she says in a warm, buttery voice that draws a head-shake and a big smile from the bartender, who moves off, leaving the man and woman facing each other.

Damn, she looks great! the man tells himself and then quickly decides to initiate a casual interaction before she looks off in another direction.

"Bombay is a great gin," he says in a tone that carries across the short distance between them but is still, he hopes, private, even intimate, so that his role as flirtatious male gets a welcoming response and he can proceed further. He gives her a big, encouraging smile.

"Yes," she says, returning his smile, displaying dazzling teeth. "I've only discovered it recently. I was always a Tanqueray fan."

"That's good, too," he says quickly, confident that an overture has been made, receptivity indicated and now that the ice has been broken, he can engage her further. He stares at her large brown eyes, warm and inviting.

"I like Gordon's, too," he says, and she makes a little frown.

"I know some people who like Gordon's, but I don't find any other gin to be as smooth as Bombay or Tanqueray," she says decisively as the bartended comes back into focus with her martini and quickly disappears from view.

"Do you like it stirred, not shaken, as James Bond always says in the movies?" he asks in a teasing tone.

"I like it dry, with only a hint of vermouth," she replies good-naturedly.

He's exhausted his small talk about gin and decides it's time to take a leap forward.

"So what's a pretty lady like you doing in the big city by herself?" he asks, wincing at the corniness of this line and covering his embarrassment with a wide grin, hoping to convey sincerity.

She takes a sip of her martini and places the glass carefully on the napkin that the bartender brought with the drink. Then she looks up at him and her brown eyes are sparkling.

"Well, maybe I live in this big city," she says, tilting her head and her soft, blond hair falls to one side. "And maybe sometimes I like to be by myself. It offers more chances for adventure."

She throws him a look, teasing and provocative. His pulse quickens.

"What about you?" she asks, and he's quick to respond.

"Oh, I'm just a tired old business man, trying to relax after a long, hard day," he says with mock solemnity.

She takes another sip of her martini and redirects her gaze to him. She lifts one eyebrow.

"You mean, before you go home to your wife and kids?"

She pauses. He smiles

"I see you're wearing a wedding ring," she says, pointing to his left hand that's wrapped around his drink.

"Yes," he admits.

"And by the way," she says, pulling the stirrer from her martini glass and popping one of the two olives skewered on it into her mouth, "that line about the lady alone in the big city is ancient. You ought to hone your pick-up skills and make them fresher, more exciting, if you want to make an impression."

"Was I trying to pick you up?" he asks teasingly.

"Weren't you?" she asks boldly, gazing directly at him.

"Well, now that you mention it, sure, I guess so."

"Good, so that's out of the way," she says matter-of-factly, popping the second olive into her mouth and rolling it around her cheeks suggestively.

"What would you suggest as a better pick-up line?" he challengers her.

"Oh, I don't know…that is, I'm not sure. Maybe just a direct compliment first; something about the lady's appearance."

Was she blushing?

"Okay, let's re-roll the tape and try again," he says. "That's a pretty dress you're wearing."

"That's no good," she says quickly. "My girlfriend could say that."

"Okay, how about 'that's a very pretty dress you're wearing and you fill it beautifully'?"

"That's better but still on the corny side," she admits. "Doesn't sound like something you'd say to a woman in 2012."

He raises his hands in mock surrender.

"I haven't had much practice at this so I guess I'm out of fashion," he says with the slightest hint of annoyance.

"Actually, I suppose it doesn't matter what line a man uses; if the woman finds him attractive, she'll respond positively." She gives him a big, affirmative smile. "Still, it adds zest to the pursuit if some clever compliments are made."

"I'll have to brush up," he concedes, and then asks, "Does it matter to you if I'm married?"

"Not at all," she answers quickly. "Why should it? I'm married, too."

He takes a sip of his scotch.

"And where's your husband tonight?"

"Oh, probably in some bar, telling some woman he's a tired business man whose wife doesn't understand him," she says without any hint of sarcasm.

"I didn't say my wife doesn't understand me."

She drops her stirrer back into her martini glass.

"You don't have to. It goes without saying that any man who's sitting in a lounge at 10 PM and starts a conversation with a lady who, I may say with no false modesty, is still reasonably attractive is not your picture of the ideal married man, contented and faithful." She takes another sip of her martini. "Am I right?" She's clearly teasing him.

"That all depends," he says, the upper part of his long body leaning across the bar at a forty-five degree angle in her direction in an attempt to span the distance between them and create more intimacy. "You're wrong about being reasonably attractive; you're damn attractive—a really great looking lady! And I am contented, very contented, in my marriage."

"But," she interrupts him, "variety is the spice of life—is that it?"

"Well," he admits, "when you've been married for fourteen years and you've got three kids, things can get a little dull."

"Especially in the bedroom," she adds, but she's still smiling. "Let me picture it. The big man of the house is tired after battling the world to make a living, and the little lady is tired after dealing with three kids, taking care of the house and running a part-time business from the home. Have I got the picture right?"

"That pretty much covers it," he says, "but they still love each other and want to rekindle that spark."

"Then maybe you two should take some time out together to rekindle that spark. Get away from the job and the kids and the chores and the daily routines and concentrate on each other."

"What would you suggest?"

"Well, maybe take a night off and go to a hotel like this and…"

"Do you think that would work?"

"I sure do!" she says decisively.

She flashes him a big smile and he's aware of her deep dimples and those flashing brown eyes and he's completely caught by her charms.

"What would you like to say to your wife if she were here right now?" she asks provocatively.

He leaves his stool, drink in hand, and moves to the stool next to hers. He's immediately aware of her subtle perfume and the smooth glow of her skin. He doesn't hesitate in answering, caught up in the challenge of the moment.

"Well, I'd tell her how much I appreciate all that she does for me and the kids, and how good she's been about keeping her bossy mother in check since she moved in with us last year."

"Okay, that's a start," she says evenly, "but it's not guaranteed to rekindle any fire."

He takes a long sip of his scotch and looks directly into her eyes.

"Then I'd tell her that not only is she the only woman I've ever loved, but that the very sight of her—her breasts, her legs, her ass, the nape of her neck, the warm, fuzzy hollow of her belly button—still excites me, and every time we do find time to make love, I'm still losing myself in her and I pinch myself for my good luck in finding her."

She puts a hand on his arm and meets his direct gaze.

"So why aren't you home trying to rekindle that spark?" she asks in a quiet, throaty voice.

He covers her hand with his and she squeezes his arm.

"Because I had a dinner meeting with business associates tonight and I have an early meeting tomorrow morning, so I'm staying in town overnight."

"Here?" she asks, boldly gazing directly at him, and he starts to feel a warm tingling spreading across his body.

"Yes."

"And if I suggested that we go to your room for a nightcap, what would you say?"

He doesn't hesitate. In short gasps of breath, he whispers in her ear.

"I'd say I was a very lucky man and call room service for a bottle of champagne."

She presses her ear against his mouth and he kisses it.

"Why don't we skip the champagne," she says, her voice matching his in urgency.

He's squeezing her hand and she's smiling luminously. Totally lost in the moment, thinking of nothing else but this hot, compliant woman, his mind already playing the X-rated tapes of things to come, he's only peripherally aware of some phone ringing in the background. They both empty their drinks and with quick finality place their empty glasses on the bar. She takes her purse and stands up. He takes out his wallet to pay the bar bill.

"Is there a Mr. Bingham here?" the bartender calls out, breaking into the intensity of the man's concentration. It takes moments before he recognizes his own name. He shifts his gaze away from her and looks down the bar, finally bringing the bartender into focus.

"I'm Bingham," he says hoarsely

"Call for you, sir." the bartender says, moving toward him with a cordless phone. He places the phone to his ear and exchanges a quizzical look with the woman as she stands frozen in place.

"Hello," he says, followed by silence as he listens to the person on the other end and she looks distracted.

"Okay, Mom, you did the right thing. We'll be there as fast as we can."

He puts the phone down on the bar and looks at her and she meets his anxious look.

"Tim's had an accident—a broken arm—and your mother took him to the emergency room."

"Oh, god!" she cries, her face collapsing into folds of worry and alarm. "We've got to get home! When's the next train?"

"At eleven-ten," he says, quickly checking his watch. "We can just make it if we get a cab."

He fumbles in his wallet, throws some bills on the bar and the bartender watches in confusion as they both rush out of the Tap Room, looking like scared children racing for cover from a lightning storm.

Exchanges: A Fairy Tale

Olga would always look back on that day and think it was either a miracle or a very bad joke. She was just putting a baby down for a nap when she glanced up and saw the couple come into the infant dormitory. She was used to people, often foreigners, being given tours of the orphanage, but they were usually interested in adopting babies or young children and she had steeled herself to give them no heed. But this couple was different and Olga couldn't help but stare. The head nurse was rattling on about something to them but Olga saw that they were returning her stare.

Olga had never seen such elegant people. The woman's blond hair was pulled back in a sleek chignon and her gray tweed suit was trimmed with dark fur at the collar and cuffs. From across the large dormitory Olga could see that the woman's face seemed smooth and pale, with large, expressive eyes and a smiling mouth. The tall man towering over the woman was distinguished not only by his exceptional height but also by his mane of curly white hair and a chesterfield coat outlining his slim frame. He carried a long umbrella that he draped by his side like a walking stick.

Sheepishly, Olga looked away as she gently rubbed the baby's stomach to produce sleep. The next minute a faint odor of some delicious scent invaded her nostrils and soft fur brushed her arm. The elegant lady, still smiling but looking intently at Olga's face, was standing next to her. Suddenly she reached out and, grasping Olga's chin gently, drew her face to within a few inches of her own. This unexpected assault threw Olga into complete confusion as she lowered her eyes and felt the blood rushing to her cheeks. Then she heard a calm, soothing voice whispering in her ear and felt a soft breath ripple across her forehead.

Olga did not understand what the lady was saying, but the tone was unmistakably kind. She summoned the courage to raise her eyes to meet the lady's stare. Now, up close, she saw that the youthful appearance from across the dormitory was belied by small creases darting around the mouth and eyes and punctuating the slim nose, but the lady's face, while past the bloom of youth, was still remarkably beautiful. In return, she seemed to be appraising Olga's face as she uttered more undecipherable words in a language that Olga guessed was English.

The head nurse and the tall gentleman had now crossed the dormitory and stood next to the elegant lady. The nurse, seeing Olga's confused embarrassment, spoke to her in Russian. "Madame thinks you're beautiful," she said in a dismissive tone. To Olga, an orphan since six months, living in a huge Russian orphanage and never hearing any type of compliment, these words were like electric shocks coursing through her body.

Having just turned fifteen, she was naturally curious about all aspects of her appearance: her body, her hair, her face. At her last physical exam conducted each year on her birthday, which was the only indication of her special day, she had reached a height of five-feet, nine-inches and towered over most of the other girls in her dormitory. Her body had finally blossomed with small, firm breasts and rounded hips and buttocks, but her face, glimpsed only in small, reflective surfaces—no mirrors adorned the premises to which she had access—was a puzzle she couldn't solve.

Olga was aware that occasionally she found other girls or even some of the matrons staring intently at her face, but she didn't know how to interpret this attention. Now, for the first time, someone was telling her that she was beautiful and this declaration was coming from a worldly lady possessed of her own beauty. A shy smile of gratitude danced across Olga's lips.

The lady released her hold on Olga's chin and turned to the man. She spoke to him while he now stared at Olga and nodded his head affirmatively, but his cool, appraising look never changed. The baby began to cry and Olga's attention was automatically drawn again to him. The nurse spoke to Olga. "Madame Wakefield wants to know how old you are."

Without looking up, Olga replied, "Fifteen," and continued rubbing the baby's stomach. Now she heard the man's voice, strong, deep and decisive, but it was fading as the couple and the nurse left Olga's side and continued their tour.

Olga began humming a soft tune to the baby, her voice having a surprisingly gay lilt reflecting her sudden state of happiness. The lady's estimation of her as being beautiful was the thought echoing in her mind and lifting her spirits beyond the drab gray of her impersonal surroundings. *I am beautiful*, she thought jubilantly. *I am beautiful!* Almost immediately, her thoughts took a forlorn turn as another inner voice said, *Who cares?*

* * * *

The next day Olga was performing her routine chores in the babies' dormitory when the head nurse again appeared and ordered her to go to the Director's office. Olga was instantly frightened since she had only seen the

Director at assemblies when all the orphans gathered in the dining hall. She had never spoken directly to the Director, a stout, elderly woman shrouded in black with closely cropped steel-gray hair and an indomitable voice; she didn't even know where the Director's office was. Plaintively, Olga voiced her confusion.

"Wash your hands and face, smooth your hair and follow me," the nurse curtly instructed. In blazing apprehension Olga quickly executed these orders and numbly followed the nurse's quick steps down several alien corridors until the nurse stopped before a massive oak door and knocked submissively. A thunderous voice commanded the knocker to enter, but the nurse opened the door, stepped aside and abruptly pushed Olga forward.

The room was large and sparsely furnished with a desk, a few straight-back chairs and a fireplace ablaze with a ferocious fire. Olga was struck by the room's warmth as compared to the consistently chilly temperatures that pervaded every other section of the orphanage. The Director looked surprisingly small seated behind her massive desk, but Olga's attention was drawn to the elegant couple from the day before. The lady was seated in one of the chairs while the man stood behind her. The lady wore the same soft, inviting smile while the man displayed only a quizzical stare.

"Come in, Olga. Sit down!" the Director said, bristling with impatience but breaking into a slight smile betraying her dissonant voice.

Olga, whose limbs seemed to be rattling uncontrollably, jerked her body forward and settled her focus on the elegant, smiling lady in a frantic effort to reassure herself that she was not about to be punished for some unknown offense. She stood rigidly by the one empty chair, not daring to sit in such august company.

The Director cleared her throat and in a harsh, clipped staccato began to speak. "Mr. and Mrs. Wakefield are here from London and have expressed an interest in adopting you. Mind you, this is just a preliminary stage, but if everything is approved, you should consider yourself a very lucky girl. It's very seldom that girls of your age are adopted. You should be very grateful."

The Director cleared her throat again as if putting a final punctuation on her little speech and sat back in her chair. During her remarks, Olga had never taken her eyes from the elegant lady who kept nodding her head and smiling encouragingly. The word ***adopting*** leaped out in dancing letters from the surrounding verbiage and echoed tumultuously in Olga's brain. Never, from the time she was six, had she ever hoped to hear that word in reference to her, having been passed over by so many visiting strangers in her earlier years; strangers who preferred blond, blue-eyed children to her exotic looks with velvet black hair and sharp brows arching coquettishly over green eyes and accentuating a slim nose.

Having abandoned all hope of escaping the orphanage until she turned eighteen, she was miraculously being selected by this elegant and clearly well-to-do couple for salvation. In nervous exaltation she giggled, followed, for the first time in many years, by an explosive bout of laughter. The lady rose and hugged her as their commingled joy erupted in exultant squeals reverberating across the room, to the clear displeasure of the Director who cleared her throat in protest. The husband remained impassively mute.

In the midst of such jubilation, Olga gave no thought as to why, at this late date, she had finally been selected

* * * *

More good news came after a few weeks when Olga was again summoned to the Director's office and brusquely told that the paperwork had been completed and the Board of Directors had approved Olga's adoption.

"You are extremely lucky," the Director exclaimed, clearly befuddled by this chain of events. "The Wakefield's are very rich and you will have a very good life. Try to be grateful. Why they ever...." The Director broke off in mid-sentence and dismissed Olga with a peremptory hand gesture.

The news of Olga's extraordinary good fortune swept across her dormitory and all the girls now regarded her with both curiosity and awe. She could sense their confusion over her being selected: why she with her gangling height and shy ways and dark features? She didn't care. She kept thinking of the elegant, smiling lady and how she had said that Olga was beautiful. She was escaping this colorless prison with its bad smells, bad food, monotonous drudgery, sullen, friendless inmates and indifferent overseers and beginning a new life of endless, undiscovered possibilities. The Wakefields' being rich was just another wonderful dimension of her new parents that she wasn't sure how to interpret until a large package arrived shortly before she was scheduled to leave the orphanage.

"These are the clothes you are to wear when you leave," the matron who had delivered the package to Olga's dormitory announced. Olga opened the package and grew misty as she discovered finery like nothing she had ever seen: a beautiful wool dress and fitted coat, a fur hat and muff (it was still cold outside in the early spring), soft leather boots and undergarments of a fabric whose delicate texture she had never felt before. She repeatedly examined one item after another, disbelieving they were really for her, until the matron said harshly, "Put those things away until next Sunday!"

Olga now knew that in just four days, she would be gone. She happily complied with the matron's command. Somehow, she endured the remaining few days, dreaming of her life to come but having difficulty in forming pictures due to her exclusive world of the drab Moscow orphanage.

Finally, Sunday came and, dressed in her sparkling new clothes which left the other girls dumbfounded, Olga was escorted by the Director, herself, to the front gate of the orphanage where a long black car was waiting at the curb. The rear door opened and a pair of arms swathed in fur reached out toward her. Unhesitatingly, Olga rushed into them. The liveried chauffeur closed the door and the car soon sped away. Olga never looked back.

* * * *

Olga would forever remember every detail of those first days of her new life at the beautiful hotel in Moscow that had formerly been a prince's palace: the tastes and varieties of rich foods, so different from the steady diet of sodden vegetable stews with occasional fatty meats served at the orphanage: the abundance of tantalizing desserts from which she was free to choose any she wished; the wallpaper and drapes and plush carpeting of her bedroom—her very own bedroom—not a shared bunk with another girl; the way the hotel staff bowed and quickly fulfilled every order given by the elegant lady.

Olga had been driven directly to the hotel where she found more boxes of beautiful clothes arranged on her bed. A Russian woman who worked as a tour guide for American tourists was also present in the multi-room hotel suite. She explained to Olga in Russian that she had been hired full-time to serve as an interpreter for Olga and Mrs. Wakefield and to begin English lessons with Olga.

Echoing the sentiments expressed by the Director, the translator, whose name was Catherine, whispered to Olga, "You are very lucky to be adopted by the Wakefield's who seem very nice and are very rich. Your life from now on will be like a fairy tale." Since no one had ever read fairy tales to Olga, Catherine's reference was obscure, and she never could have dreamt that her life would make such a sudden, dramatic shift.

Catherine also explained to Olga that they would be staying at the hotel for only a short time until they all flew back to London in Mr. Wakefield's private plane after he concluded some business in Moscow.

The only disappointing note in this miraculous new adventure was when Catherine informed Olga that Mrs. Wakefield was called Mariella and Mr. Wakefield's first name was Grayden and that they had instructed Catherine to share with Olga their wish to be called by their first names. Olga's fleeting frown revealed her disappointment at not being able to call them by parental names. She had already gaily rehearsed doing this, with both wonderment and relish.

The biggest surprise came when Catherine told Olga that the Wakefield's had decided that a change of name for Olga would be nice as she started her new life with them. They had selected Alexandra as her new name: Alexandra Wakefield. Olga digested this news with some confusion but, as she repeated the new name to herself, she felt it had a wondrous quality and sounded somehow appropriate for her new station in life. Olga of the orphanage was gone and Alexandra of the world was replacing her. She readily adopted it. At first shyly but then with greater ease, she addressed Mariella by that name and loved the way Mariella pronounced Alexandra with an English lilt that sounded soft and refined.

During those first few days while they remained in Moscow, Alexandra saw little of Grayden Wakefield, and, on those rare occasions when he would appear late at night after she and Mariella had finished dinner, she never dared to address him directly. For his part, he seemed to always be preoccupied, displaying an immobile expression, as Mariella reported on the activities of the day.

Alexandra's English lessons with Catherine had begun on the second day, and Alexandra was required to display the few English expressions she had learned. Shyly, she would say, "Hello...Please...Thank you," and "My name is Alexandra." Grayden listened, never changing his expression, and when he looked directly at Alexandra, his penetrating stare inexplicably frightened her.

After one week they left Russia and Alexandra had her first exhilarating plane ride in Grayden's private plane. She saw how the pilot, co-pilot and flight attendant, like the people at the Moscow hotel, all treated Grayden with the greatest respect. He must be a very important man, she decided with a mixture of awe and trepidation. These thoughts soon vanished as she thought eagerly of her life to come in London.

* * * *

The Wakefield house in London was a huge Edwardian stone mansion with more rooms than Alexandra could count. It was staffed with a legion of servants dedicated to ministering to the needs and whims of Mariella and now Alexandria. Grayden was gone from early morning to late evening, appearing seldom at dinner.

Entire days were spent on shopping forays to exclusive stores and couturiers where Mariella selected more new clothes for Alexandra. "We're going to make you the most beautiful girl in London," she often said gaily. Alexandra was taken to plush beauty salons where ointments and special scrubs were applied to remove any traces of acne or dark spots. "Grayden loves a flawless complexion," Mariella said as she and Alexandra surveyed the magical results of the latest treatment.

Catherine remained with Alexandra, and her English improved rapidly with daily lessons and endless opportunities to practice newly acquired words and syntax. In addition to Catherine, a tutor, music instructor, art instructor, dance instructor and a very genteel lady named Ms. Pimn who taught social graces were all hired to help Alexandra overcome the educational deficiencies of her first fifteen years. Alexandra proved to be a good and disciplined, if not brilliant, student, and she often heard her various instructors giving good reports on her progress to Mariella "My husband will be so pleased," was her frequent response.

Mariella's personal fitness trainer included Alexandra, at Grayden's command, in the private workout sessions. "We must constantly work to keep our bodies fit and supple," was a mantra Mariella often repeated before adding "even at your young age."

Grayden traveled constantly on business, and on longer trips he wanted Mariella, but not Alexandra, with him. She was left to Catherine's general supervision as her rigorous regimen of classes and workouts continued. Catherine was also charged, as part of Alexandra's education, with taking her to museums, concerts, operas, ballet recitals and the theater, all of which enthralled the teenager. Mariella would call every evening from wherever she and Grayden were staying, and Alexandra would give her long, delightful descriptions in halting English of what she had done and seen that day.

In this manner the days and months advanced rapidly until nearly three years had passed and it was Alexandra's eighteenth birthday. Catherine had recently returned to Russia and the other instructors had been dismissed, for the Wakefield's had determined that Alexandra's education was now, for their purposes, complete. Alexandra had grown fond of Catherine but dared not offer any opposition to any decision that Grayden or Mariella made.

As she stood before a full-length mirror in her bedroom, admiring the gown that Mariella had selected for her to wear at the celebratory dinner party that the staff was preparing downstairs, a wistful mood suddenly descended on Alexandra. The life of extravagance and luxury that had enveloped her since leaving the orphanage in Moscow had also been a life of isolation in which she had never been allowed to develop any friendships with other teenagers or even adults beyond the tight circle of paid employees surrounding her. Grateful for the unbelievable transformation that her life had undergone and loving Mariella for her affectionate attention, still she felt strangely cocooned and cut off from the wider world of people.

Catherine had once remarked to her that the Wakefield's had specifically instructed her not to foster Alexandra's cultivation of friends her own age. By way of explanation, Catherine noted that Mariella had said, "Alexandra's future is already planned for her and is to be different from other girls her age." Recalling this comment left Alexandra to ponder the meaning of this planned future about which she had, until now, never given any thought.

Alexandra's pensive mood was interrupted by a knock at her bedroom door. Before she could respond, Mariella entered the room, carrying a small jewelry case which she placed on a night table. Opening it she took out a delicate necklace of diamonds and sapphires and with a warm smile, came forward and stood behind Alexandra so that the two women's faces were almost fused in the mirror's reflection: one exquisitely blond and the other a breathtaking brunette, both with opalescent skin and perfect features.

Delicately placing the necklace around Alexandra's neck, Mariella spoke in almost a whisper. "Grayden wanted me to give this to you. It was the first gift he gave me when I was just the age you are now."

Hearing these words Alexandra realized that, despite all the conversations she and Mariella had shared, she had no knowledge of Mariella's past. "You mean you were eighteen when you met Grayden?"

Mariella chuckled softly. "Yes. I was enrolled in a commercial high school, when Grayden's wife came to dedicate a new wing that one of Grayden's companies had underwritten.

"Grayden's wife?"

Alexandra was staring in confusion at Mariella through the mirror. Mariella continued smiling while adjusting the necklace on Alexandra's neck. "Yes, his first wife, Aletta. I was in a long line of girls to shake her hand. She grasped both my hands. 'You're lovely,' she said and asked my name. The next day I was told that she had made inquiries about me and wanted me to come and work for her as a personal assistant. Since I didn't like school that much and my home life with a drunken father and no mother was miserable, I gladly accepted. She taught me everything about the world and I loved her."

"But then you married Grayden," Alexandra said, surprised to hear the sharpness in her tone.

"Yes, dear, but that was the way it had been planned," was Mariella's unruffled reply.

"Planned?" Confusion was clearly visible on Alexandra's face quickly supplanted by alarm as she recalled Catherine's telling her how Mariella had said that Alexandra's future was already planned and was to be different from that of other girls.

Mariella took a few steps back and surveyed Alexandra through the mirror. "You are truly beautiful. I'm so proud of you. You're everything I hoped for."

Not to be deterred, Alexandra almost shouted "How planned?"

Mariella's calm gaze never left Alexandra's face. "Planned that I should be Grayden's second wife. Just as it's been planned that you should be his third."

Paralyzed with astonishment, Alexandra could only stare fixedly at Mariella's soft smile through the mirror and in a trembling voice exclaim, "I don't understand."

"It's really quite simple," Mariella replied, taking hold of Alexandra's shoulders and turning her away from the mirror so that the two women were now facing each other. "Grayden is not like other men. He doesn't follow rules; he makes them. His views on marriage are a perfect example. He is, by nature, monogamous, but he recognizes that most marriages grow stale after a certain time. Consequently, he doesn't see marriage as a life-long commitment but as a contract with time limits. It's all very legal and proper. You sign a prenuptial contract for ten years, at the end of which time, if Grayden wants to terminate the marriage, you have already agreed to depart and he settles a very generous, stipulated amount of money on you that allows you to live in luxury for the rest of your life, provided you don't remarry. If he wishes to continue in the marriage, there are three-year options, with additional sums for each optional period.

Mariella paused, searching Alexandra's face for recognition of what she was saying but all she saw was a dumbfounded stare so she continued in a light tone.

"Grayden's first wife, Aletta, was married for sixteen years and then she selected me to replace her and now happily lives in the south of France in a beautiful chateau. It might seem strange for a wife to select her replacement but if you think about it, it's not strange at all. Grayden is a loyal but demanding man, and who knows him better and all his preferences and dislikes than his present wife? You see how he surrounds himself with beauty in his homes, furnishings, art, books and all his collections. He greatly admires beauty in women, too, and can afford to select young girls with natural beauty and then groom them to fit his needs. Aletta selected me and I selected you. If you think about our backgrounds, Alexandra, we are living a Cinderella life. We're the lucky ones."

Alexandra was now sufficiently steeped in fairy tales—they being some of the first stories Mariella had read to her in English—to understand the rags-to-riches reference. Her thoughts now drifted back to the comments of the Director and Catherine and how lucky she was to be taken in by the Wakefield's. Yet there was a growing revulsion in the pit of her stomach and she felt she was going to be sick. Mariella was still smiling reassuringly but Alexandra saw this smile as hollow, if not completely false.

"How long has your contract lasted?" she asked stonily.

"Grayden and I have been married for thirteen years," Mariella replied matter-of-factly. "Thirteen wonderful years! I have no regrets."

"But what if a wife wanted out of the marriage before a contractual period was up?"

"Then, according to the prenuptial contract, she receives s stated amount for each full year she was in the marriage and nothing else. Believe me, the difference in benefits between breaking the contract and abiding by it is immense."

"That doesn't seem quite fair," Alexandra said.

"It's his money; he makes the rules."

"You make it sound like it's strictly a business arrangement."

"It's much more than that," Mariella said in a bored tone, "but money is undeniably part of the deal."

Another question popped into Alexandra's head and she blurted it out. "And how old is Grayden?"

"Grayden will be sixty next month," Mariella answered in the same weary tone.

"That's a forty-two-year difference!" Alexandra exclaimed, barely concealing her astonishment.

Mariella's response seemed rehearsed. "With men like Grayden, age is immaterial." She turned and walked to the night table where she picked up the jewelry case and headed for the door. Turning again, she said, "Grayden and I would like to settle the terms of your marriage contract quickly since our plans are for me to leave next month. I'll be settling in New York." Her voice sounded tiny, like a child's, as she added, "I've always wanted to live in New York and I've found a beautiful brownstone just off Fifth Avenue in the East Sixties." She received still more blank stares from Alexandra and she quickly said, "Your birthday party will be starting soon so hurry down. Grayden is waiting. You look beautiful. He'll be so pleased. He plans to take you on a long honeymoon to Asia where, of course, he'll do a little business, too."

The mention of Grayden's name in conjunction with a honeymoon brought a flurry of new thoughts to Alexandra's conflicted mind. This man, who had always appeared so cool and distant, so lordly and disdainful, was now proposing to be her sixty-year-old husband. Everything she had experienced these last three years that had led to her total transformation was all a preparation for this declaration—this bargain. Her "planned future" was now fully recognized and assured. All she had to do was descend the marble stairs, wearing the diamond and sapphire necklace and, like Cinderella, the ball would begin. Wealth, position and security would be guaranteed.

Alexandra looked at herself again in her full-length mirror and grimaced. *Unlike Cinderella*, she thought, *I'm not in love and am not loved in return. I'm a commodity that my merchant price has shrewdly paid for.* Her green eyes were becoming vivid, misty pools as she reflected on her eighteen years of living during which, at both the orphanage and in her regal cloister, she had never experienced being loved. Tonight, she could seal her fate and forego love for all the material advantages the world could offer. But now, that absence of love left such a hunger in her heart that she could not deny its corrosive effect. Without it she felt she would shrivel to a mere husk of a human being, possibly resplendent on the outside but angrily crying for nourishment inwardly.

So basic a human need as love, enjoyed by the humblest to the highest, could not be permanently missing from her life, she decided. She now saw all of Mariella's soft smiles and gay attitudes as valiant efforts to mask her incompleteness.

Still gazing at her image in the mirror while her thoughts tumbled about, at first in random order but gradually in a coherent pattern, she resolved what she must do. Removing the necklace and placing it on her dressing table, she hastily changed into a dress and coat and packed a small suitcase with essentials. Mariella had always been generous in giving Alexandra spending money, and she now deposited her accumulated funds, sufficient for the first stage of emancipation, in her purse and tiptoed to the top of the marble staircase.

She heard voices coming from the dining room but she saw that the large entrance hall was empty. Her pulse quickened and her breath was suspended as she stealthfully descended the grand staircase. She reached the massive front double doors without being discovered. She opened one of the doors and stepped out into the cool night air. Now she took a deep breath and felt that the air was somehow different, more exhilarating than any breath she had ever drawn before.

She walked briskly, with a resolute step, away from the looming shadows of the Wakefield mansion and the cold, claustrophobic life it encompassed. With every step away from her past she felt more positive, more confident and more alive. This would be her second new beginning, she mused, and she vowed that her life's adventures this time would certainly include love in its fullest dimensions. Clear-headed and open to all possibilities, she began to hum a lullaby she had sung to the babies at the orphanage. She had never felt happier.

Life Support

"I bet you didn't know that I'm dead," Peter Stroud announced after taking his usual place at our table in the dining hall. Of course, the four of us seated with him, being the merry band of Longwood Retirement Village pranksters that we are—naturally, since we're all over seventy, our merriment is restricted to the verbal kind—couldn't resist this invitation.

"You could have fooled me," O'Reilly said.

"I bet you didn't know that I have gas," said Cohen

"We know! We know!" said Romero

"Perhaps the rumors of your death are greatly exaggerated," I said, proud of my clever allusion to Mark Twain.

"Thank you, Professor Caxton," Cohen said, catching my reference

"No, guys, I'm serious," Peter said, although he still had a half-smile on his face.

Drawing a piece of paper from his pocket, he continued. "I got this letter from Medicare stating that the last series of tests I had were not being paid for because I was officially listed on their records as having died one month before the tests were given."

"Then why did they send you the notice?" O'Reilly asked. "The postal service is good, but not that good."

"Maybe they have a new motto," Cohen said, "In Rain and Sleet and Snow and Beyond the Grave."

"No," Peter said. "They sent it to my estate."

"The way they exaggerate everything today," I said. "Peter's twelve-by-fifteen room is considered an estate."

"I called the Medicare number," Peter continued, "and, of course, I got a menu that listed forty different reasons for calling but none dealing with not being dead, so I kept saying 'other' after each phone prompt and then I had to listen to some trashy piece of music, interrupted every thirty seconds by a recorded voice apologizing for the delay and telling me how important my call was to them, and...."

"As important as fleas are to a dog," O'Reilly interrupted.

"...and they'd be with me in just a moment," Peter continued. "Well, after the third time I heard this recording, I decided to keep a tally of how many times it was repeated and my actual count was twenty-seven times."

"They plan it that way," Cohen said. "If you're not dead when you began the call, you will be before they get to you."

"Were you always this cheerful with your legal clients?" Romero asked.

"No," Cohen shot back. "Sometimes I told them they were guilty as hell and should expect a stiff sentence."

"What compassion! What empathy!" I said and Cohen chuckled.

"So what did they tell you?" O'Reilly asked Peter.

"I finally got to speak to some lady and she looked up my records and told me I was listed as dead. I said, 'How can that be when I'm speaking to you? Do you honestly believe I'm a ghost?' She took offense at this. 'Sir,' she said curtly, 'our records indicate that you are dead, and you should contact Social Security which has sent us this notice.' Then she said the damnedest thing: 'Social Security will pay death benefits.'"

Sally, our favorite waitress approached our table and we ordered our usual round of cocktails and then returned our attention to Peter's problem.

"You should write your congressman," Romero suggested.

"A lot good that would do," O'Reilly snorted. "Once they get elected they're dead, too—at least to the public."

"No, wait! There's more!" Peter shouted, waving his arms for silence. "I called Social Security and went through the same song and dance: 'Be patient, only a little longer, if you know your party's extension,' etcetera, and then when I finally got someone, she told me that I couldn't claim a death benefit because I was alive, and since I was alive, I should contact Medicare. 'But you've listed me as dead,' I shouted, and then this lady also took offense and said I should speak to her supervisor, and she put me on hold and after a few minutes the phone went dead and I get that goddamn recorded message, 'If you'd like to make a call, please hang up and dial again.' Now I don't know what the hell to do next."

Frustration was clearly visible on Peter's face as he finished the story of his bureaucratic dealings.

"I can think of one bright spot in this snafu," I said, hoping to raise Peter's spirits.

"What's that?" Peter asked, obviously pessimistic.

"You don't have to pay any more taxes!" I said jubilantly.

"That's right," Cohen chimed in. "You can tell the IRS that since one government agency has declared you dead, you must be treated equally by all other agencies— that's the fair American way!"

"Suppose we all write letters stating that we know for a fact that you're alive," Romero suggested.

"I'm not sure about that," O'Reilly said.

"Well, we know he comes alive at dinner time, anyway," I said.

"And he came alive when he was dancing with Mrs. Schwartz at our Valentine's Party," Cohen said, flexing his index finger and snickering.

"That was just an illusion of life," Romero said.

"Seriously, guys, there must be something we can do," I said, trying to control my laughter.

"It wouldn't do any good," Peter said. "When I offered to send my passport, birth certificate and driver's license, the lady said that would only prove that I was alive when those documents were issued."

"I could design a very official-looking Certificate of Life on my computer," I offered.

"No good," Romero said. "The government frowns on counterfeit documents."

Then Cohen did a very wise thing and asked to see the letter from Medicare. Peter was still holding it in his hand and passed it quickly to Cohen who examined it silently.

"Peter, what's your social security number?" Cohen asked. As Peter recited it, Cohen wrote it down on the bottom of the Medicare letter.

"There's your problem!" Cohen said with a glimmer of triumph in the old lawyer's voice.

"What?" we all shouted in unison.

"They changed one number. You said '887' and they have 877. There must be a Peter Stroud with a very similar social security number who died and got replaced in their records with you."

We all broke out in laughter and congratulated Cohen on finding the error, and then we congratulated Peter on not being dead. Sally arrived with our drinks and we toasted one and all on still being alive.

Mother Love

When Ellen came to live with her mother and grandmother for the first time in 1968, she was seven, her mother Theresa was twenty-five and her grandmother, called Nana, was of indeterminate age. So novel to Ellen was the idea of living with family, with blood relatives, what everyone else might have taken for granted, that she spent most days in a heightened consciousness of her new life and studied her mother and grandmother, intent on pleasing them and safeguarding her happy state.

Ellen's joy was mingled with fear that this arrangement—her mother's going off to work in the munitions factory each morning as the Vietnam War raged and her grandmother's taking care of their four-room attic apartment and looking after Ellen when she came home from school—would be temporary like all her previous boarding experiences. Her mother had never abandoned her and had paid for Ellen to be boarded with a series of families. But only now, with Nana's agreement to mind the apartment and her granddaughter, had a nuclear family unit finally come to pass and Ellen felt responsible for keeping them together.

During their first year of living together, Ellen began to sense a growing tension between her mother and grandmother centering on men: Theresa, with her sassy figure, pretty features and vivacious personality, attracted them effortlessly and Nana, dour in her religious and social conservatism, relentlessly shooed them away.

Saturday night was the one night of the week that Theresa went out. Sometimes she would join a group of women from work, but most times it was a man who would ring the bell at the front door of the two-family house, and her mother would hurry down, her high heels making a staccato sound on the two flights of wood steps and her Shalimar perfume lingering behind her. Nana insisted that before Theresa could go out with any man, she first had to bring him up to meet the family. To this demand Theresa acquiesced, and there followed a parade of men, usually considerably older than Ellen's twenty-five-year-old mother, who climbed the two flights of stairs to face the mother lioness in her den.

Ellen's role in these encounters was marginal and rehearsed. She was called out from her room for an introduction to George, Jeff, Tom, Ed, Seth, Steve or Bob; then, after a frozen smile and sometimes a forced handshake, she was sent back to her room. But their apartment was small, the walls, thin, and Nana's aggressive questioning was loud and blunt. Her interrogation centered on the man's age—"You look older" was her standard comment no matter if the age given was early thirties, mid-thirties, or even late thirties—his job, his religion, his marital status (single was the only acceptable answer) and his current living arrangements: living with parents (preferred), living alone or living with a roommate. No matter what the man's answers were, Nana stored the information and rendered her consistently negative opinion as soon as Theresa returned from any first date. A strict curfew of midnight was always stated unequivocally by Nana before Theresa and her new beau departed, and while Ellen was always asleep when her mother returned dutifully before midnight, Nana's vehement objections to the current suitor always woke her.

"He's too old!" was usually the first salvo, and not surprising since most able-bodied men in their twenties who were not in college were away fighting the Vietnam War.

"He's not Catholic!" quickly followed in the listing of unacceptable qualities, and, indeed, it did seem as though all Catholic men of suitable age were already taken, leaving the field to Methodists, Presbyterians, Congregationalists and Jews. This last category was reserved for particular scorn as Nana condemned all Jews up through the present generation as the killers of Christ, despite recent repudiations of such charges by her church.

"Did you see his fingernails?" she'd ask Theresa. "They were filthy!"

Other negative observations about the man's personal grooming were quickly enumerated and could include "needs a haircut," "teeth were yellow," and "clothes too flashy." Nothing seemed to escape Nana's attention, and "waxy earlobes, "hairy knuckles" and "scuffed shoes" were often included in her litany of imperfections.

Lying in bed, the darkness of her room punctuated by the glimmers of light from the hall outlining her bedroom door, Ellen would listen intently to Nana's ranting monologues. Her mother's voice was seldom heard, neither in response nor protest. When Nana had exhausted her objections to the latest man, Theresa would meekly say "Okay, Mommy, I'm tired. Let's go to bed," and her shadow would momentarily block the scraps of light around Ellen's door as she passed down the hall to the bathroom, followed by Nana who would end her diatribe with one final admonition.

"This is a small town, Theresa. You have to think of your reputation. You can't make any more mistakes. Think of your daughter. Think of me!"

One of her mother's suitors was especially troublesome to Nana because he was different from the rest. Wayne Hopkins was a handsome young man, only two years older than Theresa, who worked in the same munitions factory and was supervisor of a department. He was 4-F due to a pierced eardrum, which did not inhibit his daily functioning in civilian life but precluded him from military service. A Catholic, Wayne lived with his parents in a two-family house just a few blocks away, only his parents were the owners, not renters like Ellen's family. He dressed well if "a bit flashy" for Nana's taste and drove a pale yellow Chevy Camaro convertible only a few years old. He had impeccable manners, answering Nana's intrusive questions with gracious, expansive responses and frequently using "ma'am" in his replies. After the usual interrogation before a first date with Theresa, Nana had no list of offending particulars when Theresa returned home at 11:45 and resorted to some general, intuitive dissatisfaction.

"There's something fishy about him!" was all she said several times like an incantation to ward off evil.

Wayne and Theresa dated every Saturday night for several months. Unlike her other dates who, having once been exposed to Nana's withering stares and uncomfortably personal questions, never ventured up the stairs again, Wayne always came up to their apartment and politely engaged Nana in light conversation before helping Theresa on with her coat and bidding Nana and Ellen a good evening. The Saturday following Nana's birthday, he brought her both flowers and a box of

Whitman's chocolates. While Nana always acted in a formally polite, somewhat sullen manner with Wayne, this latest solicitous gesture left her clearly disconcerted as she stiffly thanked him but said in too sharp a tone that he shouldn't have done it. Still after this incident, Theresa's freedom was occasionally extended to a Sunday afternoon's outing with Wayne, and on these occasions Ellen was often included. While Nana was also invited, she never accepted,

Seated in the rear of Wayne's convertible, the smell of leather filling her nostrils, her eyes dazzled by the chrome ashtrays embedded in the side armrests and the crisscrossing bars supporting the canvas top, Ellen listened to her mother's gay chatter from the front passenger seat and Wayne's cheerful responses as he drove them to some exciting destination. One time it was an outdoor rodeo; another time it was a baseball game between two local teams.

Most times, if the weather was mild and sunny as it was wont to be in late April, it was a park or a lake where the three of them would sit on a blanket that Wayne kept in the car's trunk. They'd eat bologna and cheese or lettuce and tomato sandwiches that Theresa had prepared and packed in a wicker hamper, along with pickles, potato salad and a thermos of lemonade. For dessert they always had oatmeal raisin cookies which Wayne and Ellen liked very much. Wayne would turn the car radio up loud and he and Theresa would do impromptu dances, sometimes inviting an ecstatic Ellen to join in. Never knowing her father, Ellen would fantasize about Wayne in that role.

After eating, they'd put everything back in the car and go off for a walk, Theresa holding both Ellen's hand and Wayne's. When Wayne's car pulled up in front of their house, Wayne and Theresa would kiss quickly before she hopped out and pushed the front seat forward for Ellen to exit. They usually found Nana at the kitchen table reading her bible, a duty she seemed to feel all good Christians should practice on Sunday.

"Oh, Mommy, you should have come with us," Theresa would say gleefully. "The park is so lovely with the flowers in bloom."

Nana would barely nod in recognition of this remark. She never inquired about details of their Sunday excursions. But when Theresa was at work, she'd grill Ellen: "What did you all talk about?" "Do you like Wayne?" "Do Wayne and your mother kiss?"

Sensing the predatory attitude behind these questions and wishing to protect her mother, Ellen would give vague, non-incriminating replies, which invariably put Nana in a sour mood. Ellen liked Wayne who treated her in a friendly, offhanded manner, but she liked him the most because of the way her mother seemed to be so happy, so animated in his presence.

One afternoon Nana and Ellen had gone grocery shopping when they encountered Mrs. Tracy, an acquaintance of Nana's from church. Greeting them as they waited their turn in the checkout line, Mrs. Tracy, who had suddenly materialized behind Nana, inquired, "How's that pretty daughter of yours?"

"Just fine," Nana said. She didn't seem to like Mrs. Tracy.

"I believe I saw her with Wayne Hopkins in that fancy convertible of his last Sunday afternoon," Mrs. Tracy said, with a faint tone of disapproval.

"Yes," said Nana, "and Ellen was with them," deflecting any hint of impropriety.

Mrs. Tracy looked at Ellen, and, tucking her head into her chin as she digested this information, continued. "Yes, Wayne's a well-spoken young man and so good looking! I know his family well. It's really a shame..." and her voice trailed off as she stared intently at Nana.

"What's a shame?" Nana asked sharply, sensing important, new information about her newest rival from Mrs. Tracy's conspiratorial gaze and solemn frown.

Mrs. Tracy moved closer to Nana until it looked to Ellen that Mrs. Tracy's lips were connected to Nana's ear.

"The divorce and all," Mrs. Tracy whispered.

"What divorce?" Nana asked in a loud voice, emitting a burst of air with her excited words, but recovering quickly. "What are you talking about?" she said quietly, turning her face to stare directly at Mrs. Tracy.

Mrs. Tracy shifted her position, moving as far away from Ellen as possible while still connected to Nana's ear.

"I guess there's no reason you'd know, being relative newcomers to town," she said with a hint of condescension. Then, taking a deep breath, she began to recite Wayne's history, clearly enjoying the dramatic information she was whispering, still audible to Ellen.

"Wayne and Shirley Oakleigh, his high school sweetheart, were married right after high school and they had a baby, a little girl who was profoundly deaf and dumb, and they separated shortly after she was born. The wife took the baby... her name was Elizabeth... such a pretty little baby but she never smiled I'm told. Anyway, Shirley took Elizabeth to live in Ohio with her aunt and uncle and the next thing I heard was that she had sued Wayne for divorce. Then about a year after that I met Shirley's mother at the church bazaar and inquired politely how Shirley and Elizabeth were doing, and the mother said that Shirley had remarried and her new husband had legally adopted Elizabeth. How Wayne felt about all this I just don't know."

Mrs. Tracy stepped back and eagerly studied Nana's face for her response. Squeezing Ellen's hand, Nana turned abruptly away from Mrs. Tracy and moved forward in the checkout line. Ellen glanced back to see Mrs. Tracy's face registering both bewilderment and disappointment before she began placing her groceries on the counter.

Not speaking at all except to say "thank you" when the clerk gave her change, Nana held Ellen tightly by the hand as they hurried home. Ellen's arm hurt from being pulled and the other arm ached from carrying a bag-full of groceries that Nana had selected for the coming week's dinners. Up the two flights of steep narrow stairs they silently rushed, both of them gasping for breath as they reached their attic apartment.

Instead of the usual routine of helping Nana to put away the groceries, Ellen was sent to her room immediately. For the next hour she heard nothing but loud noises from the kitchen as Nana banged doors and slammed pots on the stove and dishes on the table. Finally she was summoned for supper. They started to eat in total silence when Ellen heard her mother climbing the stairs. Sensing helplessly that Nana's anger would soon be fully vented at her mother, Ellen sat hunched over the table, staring at her plate and playing with the peas.

Theresa put her hat and coat away in the hall closet, then entered the kitchen and said "Hi" in a cheery voice that did not completely conceal her fatigue. Following her usual custom, she bent down and gave Ellen a kiss on the cheek and said, "How's my girl?" Ellen could barely mumble "Fine" in response, so filled was she with nervous anticipation of what was to come.

Theresa moved around the kitchen table toward Nana who had not looked up from her plate. "How was your day, Mommy?" she asked as she bent to kiss her cheek but Nana abruptly pulled away, slammed her fork down on her plate, stood up and walked away from Theresa toward the stove. As she fixed a plate for Theresa she began to talk, with her back to both of them.

"My day was not very nice, Theresa, because today I learned that the whole town is gossiping about you."

Theresa stood by the table and her smile disappeared.

"What do you mean, Mommy?" she asked in a voice that suddenly sounded very tired

"I mean that I had to hear from that terrible gossip, Mrs. Tracy, that you've been dating a divorced man, a man who abandoned his own child. That's what I mean!" Nana said, her voice rising in pitch as she banged the lid on the pot containing the peas.

Theresa grabbed the back of the chair she was standing next to, as if to stop herself from falling. Then in one fluid movement her body crumpled and slid into the chair, her arms hanging limply at her sides and her eyes staring down at the table. Nana returned to the table with the plate of food she had prepared, and, standing over Theresa's bowed head, plunked it down on the table.

"How can you do this to yourself? To your daughter? To me?" Her voice was thin and high pitched.

"What child?" asked Theresa, her eyes never leaving the table as though in a trance.

"His child, Theresa. His little girl who was born deaf and dumb and he abandoned her."

Ellen saw her mother's eyes close and her shoulders sink closer to the table.

"I know nothing about a child," she said, quietly struggling to say the words.

"And I suppose you didn't know that he was divorced?" Nana asked derisively.

"Yes, I knew about that, but they were teenagers and she divorced him," Theresa said in a monotone, her eyes now staring fixedly ahead.

"So that makes it alright?" Nana said, standing over Theresa, her words beating down like hailstones. "Tell me, where does the Catholic Church say it's alright to date a divorced man because he was married as a teenager?"

Theresa, sitting like a stone statue, gave no answer. Nana continued.

"And what about you? Remember that in the eyes of God you're still a married woman. And in the eyes of this community too!" She returned to her seat at the table, and then added, "A married woman with a child!"

"A marriage of three months," was Theresa's response, muttered in a barely audible voice of quiet desperation.

Speaking in a lower, more solemn voice, with her eyes glaring at Theresa's bowed head, Nana continued.

"Still a marriage in the eyes of the church! And after all my efforts to see that you were respectably married before Ellen..."

She paused, glancing at me, and then continued.

"Well, this is the thanks I get."

Theresa raised her arms, placed her elbows on the table and rested her forehead on her cupped hands. From Ellen's side of the table she could see that her mother's eyes were closed and tears were forming at the corners.

"He never told me about a child," she said flatly, as if to herself.

"Well, now you know, along with everybody else in the town," Nana said, slapping the table sharply for emphasis.

Ellen sat transfixed with conflicting emotions: sorrow for her mother and anger at her grandmother who was clearly inflicting so much pain. She wanted to help her mother, to soothe her, but she didn't dare move, so cowed was she by Nana's angry words and intimidating gestures. Abruptly Theresa rose from the table and went into the bedroom she shared with Nana and closed the door. Nana and Ellen sat motionless at opposite sides of the table, the overhead kitchen light throwing them in sharp relief.

"Eat your supper, Ellen," said Nana, breaking the silence with a peremptory command.

Ellen could hear muffled sobs from the bedroom, which threw her into an agony of sympathy and helplessness. Summoning more courage than she knew she possessed, she said "I'm not hungry," but her defiance did not extend to looking directly at Nana.

"Then you'll sit there until you finish it," Nana said with finality.

Ellen felt her body growing hot with anger, for she wanted to leave the table and go to her mother, hug her and tell her to stop crying. Instead she stared glumly at her plate, pushing her peas under the mashed potatoes. In the only act of loyalty she was now capable of, she vowed that she would sit there until she died before she would eat this food.

They sat in silence, while Ellen continued to push the food around her plate and Nana calmly finished her meal. Then, ignoring Ellen's sullen immobility, she got up and started clearing the table. Knowing Nana's edict was still in effect, Ellen stared stonily down, listening intently for any new sounds from the bedroom. The bedroom door opened and her mother came back into the kitchen and stood by the door, far away from Nana who was busy at the sink.

"I'm sorry, Mommy," she said in a low, halting voice, wiping her eyes with a handkerchief. "I won't see him again."

Without turning from the sink, Nana responded, "I should hope not!"

Ellen looked at her mother's face and she had never seen her look so sad, so dispirited. Her eyes, usually brimming with sparks of joyfulness, now seemed hollow, void of all light. She leaned against the wall, looking frail and defeated. Ellen couldn't stand to see her this way. Defying her grandmother, she pushed her chair back and rushed to her mother, throwing her arms around her waist and burying her head in her stomach.

"Don't cry, Mom, don't cry" was all Ellen could say over and over, while her own tears stained her mother's skirt. Theresa cupped her hands behind Ellen's head and silently pressed her daughter to her, their bodies rocking together in a slow rhythm. From the opposite side of the kitchen Nana spoke.

"Ellen, put your food in the garbage and bring me your plate. Then you can finish clearing the table." Her voice was calm and matter-of-fact, a startling difference from the angry, emphatic tones she'd been using since Theresa had arrived home. Puzzled, Ellen looked up at her mother who managed a wan smile.

""Do as Nana says, dear," she said with a gentle push.

As Ellen left her mother and moved to the table to get her plate, Theresa crossed the kitchen and stood next to Nana. Picking up a towel, she began drying the dishes that Nana had washed and placed on the drain board. The three of them now completed their tasks in silence as the tension in the room seemed to slowly evaporate. A battle had been waged, wounds inflicted, concessions won and a truce forged. In victory Nana could be magnanimous. Another rival vanquished! Rinsing the last dish and handing it to Theresa, she broke the prolonged, soothing silence.

"You haven't eaten yet," she said. I'll warm the food up."

"Thank you but don't bother. I'm not hungry," Theresa replied.

"How about a nice cup of tea and some chocolate cake?" Nana asked brightly, all traces of anger having left her.

"That would be nice," Theresa said with no enthusiasm. Then, turning to her daughter, she asked, "Don't you have homework, Ellen?"

Ellen nodded yes and headed for her bedroom where she spread out her books and papers on the bed and, lying on her stomach, tackled the evening's assignments. Nana and her mother had moved into the living room to watch the news on television, and Ellen could hear their casual comments about the news items being reported, as a peaceful routine once again settled over their household.

Later that evening, when it was Ellen's bedtime, her mother came into her room for their brief ritual of bedtime prayers. With her mother kneeling at her side, Ellen finished her list of people to ask God's blessings on and thanked Him for special blessings. She quickly said "Amen," made the sign of the cross and hopped into bed.

Her mother tucked the covers around Ellen's chin and bent down to kiss her cheek. Then in an uneven voice that sounded as if she were very far away and suddenly very old, she said, "Say a special prayer for me, Ellen." The child gazed up at her mother and saw that although she was smiling, there were new tears glistening at the corners of her eyes.

Angel's Baby

This is a New York story. It could have taken place in other cities, but, let's face it, no other city equals New York for its urban myths and legends, its gargantuan sweep of characters, its placid tolerance of the flamboyant. New Orleans is the only other city that even comes close, but New York still tops the list since it's so much bigger, and outrageousness is so much more widespread. And since the characters in this story are the most outrageous you could possibly imagine, their setting has to be New York, in Spanish Harlem on a hot August night around 2 AM.

A party has been going on since the late afternoon in a dilapidated old brownstone row house and it shows no signs of stopping. The pounding Salsa music is blasting into the street, but no one seems to mind since this is a party that everyone is invited to, and for hours there's been a steady stream of people up and down the worn front steps, all dressed up, laughing and smiling and greeting friends with excited shouts and dramatic hugs.

The party is to celebrate the birthday of Baby, the biggest celebrity in this poor, crowded neighborhood where Spanish is the main language and everybody hustles to make a buck. Madame Yolanda, reader of cards, tea leaves and palms, lives on the first floor. Jose Pitura, who runs an illegal gambling operation, lives on the second. And Baby lives on the two upper floors with his family.

Baby's family consists only of very pretty women between the ages of eighteen and twenty-five, and they keep changing. Baby is in his early thirties, tall and slender, with piercing black eyes set off by carefully shaped, swooping black eyebrows, shellacked black hair and a smile that displays his strong white teeth and his dimples to irresistible advantage. Because he was the youngest child and only boy in a large family, his sisters all called him Baby, and, as he grew to manhood, the name stuck. So secure was he in his masculinity and his appeal to women that he embraced this nickname for the contradiction it presented.

The girls in Baby's family all love him and vie for his attention. Like some sultan from the Arabian Nights, he measures out his affection depending on his mood or whim, as well as the money they contribute each night to his upkeep, which keeps his family in a constant state of uncertainty, agitation and eagerness to please. Fights among the girls periodically erupt but Baby, who is gentle and sweet by nature, can also be stern in administering discipline. Stories are told about the nasty things that have happened to members of Baby's family who have displeased or disappointed him. It's understandable why the girls both love and fear him. In this way order and harmony are maintained. Until recently.

For all the gaiety of the party, there is more unease just under the surface than anyone can remember. The girls have spent lavishly from their allowance that Baby doles out to them, competing to see who can give him the best birthday present. They have taken extra time with their hair and makeup and are wearing their flashiest, most provocative outfits. Still, as soon as Angel arrives, Baby has eyes for no one else.

Everyone agrees that they have never seen Baby act this way before and they watch enviously as he dances dance after dance with Angel and whispers things in her ear and feeds her from the elaborate buffet and then takes her off to a corner for a private chat. Some of the girls in Baby's family start to pout; others look angry or sit in sullen silence, watching every move that Baby makes and critically appraising Angel's dress, hair, makeup and figure.

Now here's where the outrageous twist to this story begins.

Angel had arrived in the neighborhood just two months earlier from Puerto Rico where, in the bohemian demimonde of San Juan she was known as an extremely beautiful young woman who had once been acknowledged to be the most beautiful boy in the entire island.

So powerful was the impact of Angel's perfectly sculptured features, porcelain skin, huge dark, almond-shaped eyes and precipitously high cheekbones, framed with thick curly chestnut hair, that even as a boy, people would stop in the street, their mouths agape, drinking in his beauty. With a small-boned, delicate body and a natural sweetness that pervaded all his actions, it was easy to mistake him for a girl—an extremely beautiful girl.

When, at the age of thirteen, he defied his mother—his father was dead—and let his hair grow long as well as affecting a unisex style of dress, the outer transformation to the opposite gender was complete.

It is appropriate at this point, in keeping with Angel's new identity, to change pronouns. Since Angel was a man's name in Spanish, pronounced an-hell, giving it the Anglicized pronunciation, an-gel (like the heavenly spirits), was an easy adaptation. And since most people described her as having the face of an angel, it seemed most appropriate.

By the time she was fifteen Angel had left her mother and was living with a much older man, a wealthy lawyer, who worshipped her as a prized possession, an object of beauty to be admired and savored. This wealthy lawyer was neither a pedophile nor a homosexual. He wanted Angel to undergo gender realignment surgery as soon as she turned eighteen, but except for some silicone injections to create breasts and feminine hips, Angel was so fearful of the knife and the pain associated with this major operation that she refused.

The lawyer begged, pleaded, wheedled, cajoled and, finally, threatened. Angel stubbornly resisted. So heated did their home atmosphere ultimately become that Angel took all the pretty clothes and jewelry he had given her, stuffed them into three Louis Vuitton suitcases and escaped to New York City, taking refuge with a cousin.

Shortly after her arrival, Angel's appearance on the streets of Spanish Harlem caused a buzz in the community about the very beautiful young girl who had suddenly appeared among them. Baby heard about this rare beauty and, always interested in recruiting new members to his family, went to investigate. He saw her coming out of a cantina with her cousin, Inez, whom he knew slightly. Since everyone knew Baby, he walked right up to Inez and this breathtaking creature to say hello.

Angel and Baby exchanged glances and, as the epitome of feminine beauty and daintiness met the personification of virile handsomeness, it was love at first sight. Angel blushed and Baby was momentarily tongue-tied. From that moment on, he ardently pursued her, not as a star attraction in his family but as his private soul mate and prized possession.

When, on their second evening together, Angel explained her unusual situation, Baby was surprised by his own response: shocked that this gorgeous creature, in her appearance and demeanor, gave no hint of anything amiss—even her voice was soft and fluttery—but, like the lawyer in Puerto Rico, immediately eager to help her complete the transformation so he could possess her entirely. He offered to bankroll the entire procedure and Angel, being of a romantic disposition, now loved him more for his generous acceptance.

Baby was used to women falling in line with his desires and was eager to have Angel undergo the surgery now that she had turned eighteen. Poor Angel, caught between her ripening romantic love for Baby and her great fear of the surgeon's knife, was plunged into a vortex of conflicting emotions and kept procrastinating. Baby's insistent urgings, until the night of his birthday party, had been models of delicacy, but after several weeks of such promptings, his dominant, authoritarian side, fueled since the start of the party with much tequila, was now clearly on display.

The ladies in Baby's family, who know nothing about Angel's real condition, now watch enviously the tête-à-tête between their beloved pimp and this resented interloper. They could never have guessed what the subject of their intimate conversation is about. Loosely translated from the Spanish, it goes like this.

"Adorable one, I want you more than I've ever wanted any other woman. I want you to be my lady."

"Are you proposing, Baby?"

"Well, yes, but I can't wait."

"But I'm afraid."

"There's nothing to be afraid of. I'll get you the best doctors and the best care."

"But the pain!"

"Sweet lips, drugs can take care of any pain."

"But I've heard of surgeries that were botched."

"You'll have nothing but the best that money can buy, I swear on my mother's grave. Just leave it to me. But you've got to do it right away. This is driving me crazy."

And so the conversation went, until Angel, distraught with conflicting emotions, rushes from the party and down the stairs, with Baby in hot pursuit. He catches up with her at the front door of the brownstone. At this point their exchanges take the form of a heated argument, with Baby insisting that she must, and Angel crying that she can't. The curious onlookers have no idea what the point of this angry confrontation is, but they have never seen Baby so furious, or any girl in his company so defiant.

Finally, in a blind rage of frustration and humiliation, feeling that his masculine authority is being compromised and fueled with much too much tequila, Baby losses all reason and, avoiding that beautiful face, punches Angel in the stomach, delivering so fierce a blow that she lurches backwards and tumbles down the eight front steps of the building.

Angel lies on the sidewalk and is quickly surrounded by a small crowd. Still in a white hot rage, but also feeling embarrassed to have so many onlookers witness his mean side, Baby races back upstairs to his apartment, rushing through the rooms where the party is going full blast, and locks himself in his bedroom to cool off.

Meanwhile, Angel still isn't moving and someone calls 911 and an ambulance soon arrives with an emergency medical team. They see that this beautiful young woman is breathing but unconscious and lift her into the ambulance. While speeding toward the nearest hospital, the woman regains semi-consciousness. She's clutching her stomach and moaning "baby, baby, baby."

The EMTs immediately assume they've got a woman in the early stages of pregnancy who might be suffering a miscarriage.

The ambulance soon arrives at the hospital and Angel is wheeled into the emergency room where a doctor on duty begins his examination. Angel is now fully conscious and thoroughly frightened by her strange surroundings. She hears an EMT telling the doctor something about a baby and thinks that he somehow knows what Baby did to her and this could mean trouble for him.

As the doctor gently starts to lift her dress, Angel panics at what he'll soon discover. In a giant spurt of adrenalin she pushes the doctor's hands away, jumps from the examination table and, avoiding the clutches of the EMT, rushes wildly out into the night, screaming, "Baby, Baby, Baby."

Thus was born another New York legend of a hauntingly beautiful, young woman seen late at night racing hysterically through the streets of Manhattan, forlornly searching for her lost baby.

When The Door Slammed

I had the dream again last night. It's always so vivid, in living color and enhanced sound. Actually, it's a multi-sensory experience and I seem to hear things more acutely and see details that I wouldn't usually notice, and my feelings swell to the point of paralysis. Shock and fear come first, followed quickly by anger and frustration, and then despair and self-loathing.

I mention it to my wife over the double sink in our master bathroom as we get ready for work, and she nods, saying she knew it must have been that dream from all the tossing and shouting I was doing. She also says that she knows I'll be in a lousy mood today and, of course, she's right. I can never entirely shake off the feelings from the dream for at least twenty-four hours.

"It was more than thirty years ago, for god's sake! Why can't I ever escape it?" I ask, more confused than angry.

She pauses in the application of her mascara, her arm suspended in space next to her cheek.

"Because it's a major event in your life that you'll always carry with you, and..." she hesitates and her voice takes on a darker shade, "you'll probably never know all the ways it affects you...affects us."

I momentarily see her eyes trying to lock into mine through the mirror but I quickly glance away.

"Okay," I say, reaching for the toothpaste, annoyed. "I can live with that: carrying it inside me. I just don't want to have to relive those scenes every six months. The dream's so vivid, so real every time. It opens all the old wounds and, no matter how old I am, I have to come to terms with my feelings all over again."

She finishes her mascara maneuvers and quickly daubs lipstick on her pursed lips before responding.

"There's probably nothing you can do about that," she says matter-of-factly, pressing her lips together before adding, "except for...," but she pauses and seems to be weighing her words, then says, "except for what Dr. Roth told you."

She gives me a final look in the mirror and passes into our bedroom.

Dr. Louis Roth is the psychiatrist I've been seeing off and on for many years, beginning in my mid-twenties, shortly after I got married, when the dream started invading my sleep relentlessly and lingering with searing clarity in my waking hours. At my last session about eight months ago, Dr. Roth challenged me with a startling comment.

"It's really not a dream, Mr. Littleton!"

Dr. Roth, an austere, formal Freudian in his late sixties, always spoke in a low, deliberate voice.

"At least, not in the truest sense of our clinical definition of dream. That's when the mind, in its freest, subconscious state, scrambles seemingly unconnected facts, people and events and reorders them in some new configuration, usually with strong symbolic overtones. These symbols are open to various interpretations, one of which finally gains some objective validity by its recurring pattern among the ever-changing details."

Dr. Roth paused to let me digest this statement.

"But in your case, no matter how many times you report your dream to me and no matter how much we examine it, the details--even the smallest details--always remain the same. This suggests that your mind keeps returning to the same scene, not in an unconscious but in a semi-conscious state, and not for any symbolic rendering of the horrible events of that night when you were fourteen. Rather, there's some unresolved emotional issue that you have yet to confront, to accept and to be at peace with."

Dr. Roth shifted his weight in his leather chair and looked directly into my eyes.

"Until you reach that state, Mr. Littleton—and you must reach it by yourself—I can't be of much help."

Hearing this pronouncement, I wallowed in self-pity, but Dr. Roth continued.

'You have acknowledged, again and again, that to your best, most accurate recollection, there is absolutely no difference between the recurring dream and the actual event as stored in your memory. Furthermore, you insist that the dream omits no details of the actual event, including the emotions you experienced at that time, as you now remember them. Therefore, you must revisit it again in the fullest state of consciousness. You must examine it, if you will, like a detective, looking for the slightest bits of new evidence that you may have previously overlooked or might have unconsciously suppressed, that could help you gain some new insight. All my probing through the years of our periodic sessions has not led to that insight, and I feel I cannot be of any further help."

Closing my file that had been on his lap with an air of finality, he looked impassively through me.

"It's now entirely up to you. It's clear to me that the scene that endlessly replays itself in your mind, whether sleeping or waking, presents a puzzle that you alone can solve."

Rising from his worn leather chair, Dr. Roth turned towards his desk, his tone and actions clearly dismissing me.

"You must find the key to the puzzle, Mr. Littleton, and only then will you solve it"

Dejected, I left his office that day and have not seen him since, nor have I followed his advice and given a full, conscious examination to the scene that was haunting me, primarily because the dream had not recurred until last night. Now I'm back to square one.

I finish dressing in a totally sour mood. My wife hands me a cup of coffee when I enter the kitchen and then kisses my check and is off to work.

"Don't dawdle. You'll be late for work," she says over her shoulder as she heads out the door.

"I'm the boss, remember? I can afford to be late."

I wander over to the family room, coffee in hand, as the rising sun pokes through the shutters, illuminating our collection of family pictures on the piano: our wedding picture; our two kids in various stages from infancy to post-college adulthood; pictures commemorating major family events.

Then my eye falls on the picture that I usually try to avoid looking at—would not even have it on display if my wife did not insist, for some reason I can't fathom— because it evokes too many negative associations, too many conflictive feelings. It's a picture of me taken on my fourteenth birthday. Now, as I unexpectedly stare at it, I feel with total conviction that it betrays me to the world and that anyone examining the smiling face of the not-bad-looking adolescent could easily discern the forced smile, the self-conscious pose and the desperate look in the eyes. Eyes that tell you how much I want to please you; how eager I am to be loved again. But, also, when you look closely, eyes full of doubt and uncertainty. Then I remind myself that I see all those things because I know how I was feeling on that very day when the picture was taken. With no plan or forethought, I move aimlessly to the other side of the family room that's not yet touched by the galloping sun, and, with coffee still in-hand, sit at one end of the tan suede sofa, allowing old memories, dormant images and strong feelings to sweep over me once again.

* * * *

"A big smile now, Tom," she says as she aims the camera at me. Her name is Marion and she is my foster mother and I love her. She and her husband, Jack, and their two kids, Jerry, who is twelve, and Carol, nine, are the third foster family I've been placed with by the Child Welfare Division of New York City's Social Services Department.

I had lost my parents two years earlier when they were hit by a runaway Manhattan cross-town bus whose driver had suffered a heart attack. Slammed against the brick wall of an apartment building, my father was killed instantly and my mother died the next day. With no siblings, aunts or uncles, I was suddenly, starkly alone.

I'm considered a difficult case: "typically rebellious adolescent male, bright, brooding, sensitive and quick to anger," is how I once heard my case worker describe me after I had run away from my first foster family when they treated me like shit. The second family I was placed with wasn't much better. They saw me as a live-in servant and loaded me with so many chores that I couldn't even do my homework. Of course, when Sheila, my case worker, made visits to the home, the husband would be all smiles and tell her that he was trying to make a man of me by giving me responsibilities. When Sheila got around to asking me how I was, my sullen response clearly indicated my dissatisfaction.

"You must remember, Tom," she'd say quietly, drawing me aside, "that it's very difficult to find placements for a boy your age, so I suggest you try to get on here."

I wanted to tell Sheila that the seventeen-year-old son was using me as a punching bag and was always grabbing my crotch but her stern look told me she didn't want to hear any of this. So I said nothing and a few weeks later when the son crawled into my bed and tried to pin me down, I kneed him in the balls and his cries of pain brought his parents rushing into the room we shared. Of course, his version of the incident was entirely different from mine and, naturally, they took his side. The next afternoon, after school, I threw my clothes and a picture of my parents into a shopping bag and was gone. I went to a movie, saw it twice, and then rode the subway for hours, not knowing where to go or what to do next. I was spotted by a transit cop and was escorted to juvenile court where I had already been reported as a runaway (for the second time). Now I was back at Morisania Children's Center, since my foster family didn't want me back and Sheila had given up on me. So had I. Then a miracle happened.

A volunteer named Marion worked at the Center in what was called the library but was actually a corner of the white tiled cafeteria with a rolling cart of books. It's funny when I think back on it but what I remember most about the Center was the absence of any color-- everything was painted white, except for the long rows of black metal cots in the boys' dormitory—and the powerful smell of antiseptic everywhere. All the people in charge seemed tired and never made eye contact with me. The kids ran the gamut from bullies to bed-wetters, but I was one of the older boys and stayed pretty much to myself, absorbed in my loss of family, my dislocation and lack of hope.

Reading was my one escape. Marion and I started talking about books and we developed a friendship. She was small and thin, in her mid-thirties and very pretty. Her opalescent coloring, honey blond hair and blue eyes reminded me of my mother. Few kids were interested in reading and I always sought her out when she was alone.

"You're a great reader, Tom," she'd say, flashing me a big smile as I handed her the book I had just finished. "What did you think of *The Jungle Book?*"

"I liked it," I said, always eager to chat with her, "especially how the orphan Mowgli is brought up by wolves and becomes friends with the bear and the Black Panther who teach him lots of stuff about the jungle."

"Yes," she said, "I can understand how any boy would enjoy the adventures of Mowgli." Surveying the meager assortment on her book cart, she continued. "That's the third Kipling book in a row. Would you like to try some other author? Maybe Dumas' *The Three Musketeers?*"

"No, I'd like to try another Kipling."

A small frown raced across her face.

"I'm afraid we haven't any more Kipling." Then she smiled. "I'll tell you what I'll do," she said brightly. "I'll bring you another collection of his short stories from home, but you'll have to wait until tomorrow."

211

"No problem," I said, touched by her thoughtfulness.

The next day she had the book for me, as promised, and for months thereafter she brought me books from her home library and our friendship grew. She was the only one who treated me as an individual, who showed any interest in me, and my time with her was the highlight of any day.

Occasionally, Marion would gently ask me questions about my parents, which, because of her warm, receptive nature, usually opened the floodgates and out would pour all my memories of my happy childhood up to the time of their deaths: my mother's love of laughter and my father's quiet patience; a peaceful home life, disturbed only by my vaguely glimpsed parents' worries about money when my father, a salesman, lost a job or some big client and my mother talked of returning to work as a secretary. Marion must have read my file or heard about me from other staff members because once or twice she broached the subject of my previous unsuccessful placements.

"Why did you run away, Tom?" she asked in a neutral tone, but anger flashed across my face at the thought of being diminished in Marion's eyes because of my sullied reputation.

"Because I...because they didn't...," but the words needed to describe injustice and indifference and abuse wouldn't come and, in angry indignation, I fought back tears.

Marion instinctively wrapped me in her arms, warm and fragrant, and it had been so long since anyone had hugged me—the last time was when my mother hugged me the day before she died—I now unexpectedly felt the tears coming for the joyful comfort of this human touch.

"There now; there now," she said softly, stroking my hair. "I understand."

She released me and taking her bag from the bottom of the book cart, rummaged through it until she found a packet of tissues and handed them to me.

"Blow your nose good and hard," she said after I had wiped my eyes.

I was now sheepishly self-conscious about my unmanly display but Marion made me feel that my outburst was perfectly natural. From that moment I loved her. She came to the Center only two days a week and I lived for those days. She told me about her own two children, Jerry and Carol. One day she had a surprise.

"How would you like to meet my family?" she asked, her eyes sparkling.

"Will they come here?" I asked, feeling that this place would put me at a definite disadvantage with her kids.

"No," she answered quickly. "I've arranged to take you out for dinner next Sunday with my family. Would you like that?"

I shook my head vigorously and my face exploded into one broad smile

"Good. Then next Sunday at three. I'll arrange it," she said and we both laughed a little self-consciously.

Time slowed and dragged on interminably until Sunday at three. Marion arrived a few minutes before three and we took a taxi to an address on Central Park West where a doorman opened the door and another man behind a desk in the huge, ornate lobby said "Good afternoon, Mrs. Johnson." We entered a large elevator done in dark wood with shiny brass accents and Marion pressed the button marked "penthouse," and when the elevator door opened, we stepped out into a large marble hallway with only two apartment doors, one at each end.

I was dazzled by the size of the apartment we entered, with its many rooms and broad terraces. The living room and the adjacent library—I marveled at all the books—both had a fireplace and there were sweeping views of Central Park from just about any place you looked. This was certainly different from the small, two-bedroom walkup in Hell's Kitchen where I had been raised.

I met Marion's kids. ""This is my friend, Tom," was how Marion introduced me to her kids, and we shook hands. "Carol's nine and Jerry is just two years younger than you," she explained. "He'll be twelve on March seventeenth and you'll be fourteen on March twenty-ninth, right?"

I nodded, amazed that Marion knew my birthday.

Carol was shy and pretty like her mother. Jerry was one of the friendliest kids I had ever met, stepping forth to greet me with a wide smile.

"Let's go to my room and I'll show you my fort," he suggested immediately.

His room was very large and in one corner on a long table was the most impressive scale model castle/fort I'd ever seen, with turrets and miniature cannons and an operable drawbridge and even a flagpole with pennants. Armored knights on horseback filled the courtyard and soldiers with muskets manned the battlements. Two formations of cavalry and foot soldiers were arranged outside the fort. Jerry showed me how to lower the drawbridge and raise the pennants on the flagpole. Although I had outgrown playing with soldiers, Jerry's enthusiasm was contagious. I was so impressed with this realistic castle and the many beautifully detailed knights and soldiers on display that I hadn't noticed a man entering the room and quietly observing us.

"Oh, hi Dad," Jerry said in a low voice, looking up from where he'd been rearranging the cavalry formation, and then quickly shooting a nervous glance at me before turning his attention back to the soldiers. I now saw a very tall and powerfully built man standing just inside the doorway, with heavy brows shadowing piercing dark eyes and a concentrated look on his face. He came forward with a huge hand extended toward me.

"Hi, Tom, I'm Jack Johnson," he said with a slight smile, and I awkwardly extended my hand. There was no firmness to his handshake—a hallmark of proper masculine etiquette I had learned from my father at an early age and thereafter practiced.

"I'm showing Tom my fort," Jerry said, but all the enthusiasm had left his voice.

"That's nice," his father said off-handedly. "Dinner is almost ready and your mother says you boys should wash up."

"Okay," Jerry said quietly and led me to a private bathroom that connected to his sister's room. I glanced at the tiled shower stall and saw multiple shower jets which immediately intrigued me.

Dinner was served in a formal dining room with a long table surrounded by ten chairs under a beautiful crystal chandelier. I had never seen anything like it. A large platter of roast beef was brought from the adjacent kitchen by a heavy—my mother had told me never to use the word fat—black lady.

"Tom, this is Sarah," Marion said, as Sarah gave me a big grin.

Remembering my manners, I stood up to say hello.

"The boy has very good manners; that's obvious," commented Jack as he passed an ornately designed gravy bowl to Carol. He was seated at the head of the table with his back to a large window that looked down across the vast expanse of Central Park. Marion, passing a dish of mashed potatoes to Jerry, responded to Jack's comment by smiling warmly at me.

Jerry was an animated, uninhibited talker, and I followed his lead. Throughout dinner we pretty much dominated the conversation. We discovered that we were both ardent Yankee fans, and a lively discussion of individual Yankee players ensued between us, with Marion occasionally offering some encouraging comment.

"I thought Jerry was the only fanatic Yankee fan but, Tom, you can match him, I see."

Jack ate his dinner without joining in the conversation. I had the strong feeling that he was observing us with a curious intensity.

"How about some apple pie a la mode?" Marion asked, as Sarah was clearing the table. Recognizing my confused look, she quickly said, "Apple pie with ice cream." I never forgot that phrase or where I first heard it. My parents never used expressions like that or any fancy words, for that matter.

"And after dinner, I'll show you my baseball cards," Jerry said excitedly.

"Tom, would you like to see my room?" Carol asked in a near-whisper, evidently deciding that she'd like some of my time.

"Sure," I said, happy to be the object of so much attention.

The hours passed very quickly that Sunday afternoon and I wallowed in happiness, pretending to be part of this wonderful family, in this beautiful home. Jack had disappeared immediately after dinner, to where I did not know. The sun was casting long shadows over the park when Marion interrupted a vigorous game of ski ball that Jerry and I were playing while Carol stood by my side, urging me on to beat her brother.

"Tom, I'm sorry but I promised to have you back before seven-thirty."

All my pretending evaporated on the spot. Jerry and Carol both said in unison, "No, Mom!" but Marion just smiled and nodded yes. The two children followed Marion and me out to the elevator.

"Maybe you can go with us to a Yankee game this season," Jerry said optimistically, clearly trying to lift my spirits after seeing the glum look on my face.

"Maybe," I said with no conviction.

Jack suddenly appeared in the foyer.

"Goodbye, Tom," he said genially. "You're a credit to your parents' training."

The mention of my parents instantly cast an invidious comparison between this warm family unit and the absence of my own, and "Thank you, sir," was all I could muster. The two children and their father stood smiling at me as the elevator doors closed and my spirits plummeted more quickly than the descending car. The doorman blew his whistle for a taxi and in the ride back to the Center, Marion and I were mostly silent. I was struggling to adjust to the reality of my situation after the glorious fantasy of this afternoon. Just before we reached our destination, Marion turned to me.

"Tom, this has been a wonderful afternoon and I promise you that we'll do this again." She spoke with such quiet resoluteness that glimmers of hope penetrated my forlorn mood and momentarily revived my spirits. She walked me into the cold marble vestibule with an attendant slouching behind a desk.

"See you Tuesday," she said cheerfully and gave me a big hug. I hugged her back and was unwilling to let go of her until I felt a gentle pressure on my shoulders. I inhaled her smell and hoped it would stay with me until Tuesday, which couldn't come fast enough. I was now living eagerly for the smile, the touch, the approval of someone I could love.

* * * *

As Marion had promised, there were other Sundays and then Saturdays and then overnight stays on a trundle bed wheeled into Jerry's room where we stayed up after the lights went out, talking about baseball and school and dreams about the future—his were far grander than mime—and things we loved—I never mentioned his mother—and things we hated—the Giants and lima beans and vaccinations and girls who made fun of us.

Jerry was the kindest, most generous and warm hearted person I had ever met; our friendship flourished and we quickly became very close. I had made only one friend at the Center, Joey Cassitano, but that friendship paled in comparison to my growing bonds with Jerry.

I soon came to love them all, Marion, Jerry, Carol, even Sarah the part-time cook and housekeeper. Shy sweet Carol accepted me completely and I sensed a bit of hero worship in her attitude and gallantly responded to her calls for attention. Marion, of course, I already worshipped and all my interactions with her family only served to enshrine her higher in my adoration. It was only Jack whom I was unsure about. I learned that he was a partner, "the youngest partner at thirty-eight," as Marion told me proudly, of a large law firm dealing in corporate mergers and acquisitions. He was away from home a lot and when he was present during my increasingly frequent visits, he was pleasant but distant. Yet I noticed that he was the same way with Jerry and Carol and that they, too, seemed to be guarded with him and not as exuberant in his presence. Still, my time with the Johnsons was a magical transformation of my life and I treasured every minute spent with them.

One Tuesday Marion didn't show up at the Center and I immediately panicked, worrying that I might have unknowingly done something to offend her or her family and that she no longer wanted to see me. I remembered when I was with my first foster family and a neighbor family had invited me to go with them to a camp in the Adirondacks for two weeks, thinking I'd be a companion for their only son, Sebastian, who was my age, twelve. Everything was going along fine for the first few days but then on a rainy afternoon Sebastian and I got into a typical kids' argument when I caught him cheating at a card game we were playing. He threw his cards on the table, including the one he had kept hidden on his lap, and stomped off to our bunkroom, slamming the door. His mother, a nervous lady who seemed to be always hovering about us, hurried after him

"He's a liar! He's no fun anymore! Send him home!" I heard Sebastian say in a soggy, petulant voice.

"Dear, we can't do that. It would hurt his feelings and, besides, we told the Crawford's we'd take him for the full two weeks."

"I don't care!" Sebastian screamed. "I don't want to play with him anymore. Get rid of him!"

At twelve, Sebastian already ruled his mousy mother. I listened to his denunciations of me and felt defenseless. His mother came out from the bunkroom and gave me a wan smile before scurrying back to the kitchen to prepare dinner. Sebastian stayed in the bunkroom and I stayed glued to my seat in the living room, idly playing a game of solitaire, wondering how I could make amends. Finally, ignoring my sense of justice, I went to the bunkroom.

"Sebastian, I'm sorry that we quarreled. Let's shake and forget it."

Lying on his bottom bunk, Sebastian turned on his side facing the wall.

"Leave me alone and get out of here!" was his vehement reply and I could do nothing but retreat.

When Sebastian's father, who traveled up for weekend visits, arrived on Friday night, the tension was high. Sebastian refused to speak to me, even at the dinner table, and on Saturday he still would have nothing to do with me even when his father drove all of us to a nearby lake for swimming and a picnic. On Sunday morning the father spoke to me.

"Tom, I'm sorry but this isn't working out and you'll be driving back with me this afternoon. I've called the Crawford's and they know you're coming."

The three-hour drive to my foster family's home was made in silence as I weighed the precariousness of my position with these families and bitterly recognized the equation of my present life: a foster child must always please the people who have taken pity on him or they will cast him off.

Now I remembered that lesson when Marion hadn't shown up, but was flooded with relief at seeing her in her usual spot on Thursday. Approaching her I saw that her cheek was badly bruised. Seeing the look of concern on my face, she quickly smiled and touched her discolored cheek.

"It's nothing, Tom. I walked smack into an open cabinet door at home and now I look like I've been in a war," she joked. I was relieved and smiled back, and soon we were talking about Hemingway's *The Old Man and the Sea.*

One Sunday afternoon, after spending a wonderful weekend with Marion, Jerry and Carol, touring the Museum of Natural History, seeing the show at The Planetarium, having brunch in a restaurant and bicycling in Central Park—I used Jack's bike since he was away on business—Marion gathered all of us in the living room.

"Tom," she said, and I heard a nervous edge to her voice, "we've all grown to love you and to think of you as part of our family."

Jerry, who was sitting next to me on a sofa, flung his arm around my shoulder. "Yeah, like a brother," he said gleefully and Carol giggled. Marion continued.

"We've all discussed this and we'd like you to come and live with us full-time."

I was dumbfounded by this announcement and couldn't speak. This was too good to be really happening.

Jerry interrupted again, speaking in an excited, rapid voice. "We're gonna put twin beds in my room and you can have your own dresser and I'll share the closet and shelf space with you."

Carol said nothing but was beaming and jumping up and down with excitement.

"Would you like that, Tom?" Marion asked.

I said nothing. I felt tears welling up and knew if I tried to speak, my words wouldn't come. Marion saw my state, got up and held out her arms. I rushed into them and then Jerry and Carol were hugging my back. It was the happiest moment I had ever known and I felt that I was really part of a family again, that I belonged, that I loved and was loved, that I had worth.

* * * *

It was an easy adjustment to my new life, although my wonderment at my extraordinary good fortune was endless. I was enrolled in Jerry's private school, two grades ahead of him, and we walked to and from school together, like two real brothers. Among my school peers I quickly gained a reputation for being smart and, since I was willing to help other kids who struggled with schoolwork, friendly. With Jerry's naturally easy-going personality and my sustained euphoria at my good fortune, Jerry and I never quarreled or fought and became truly each other's best friend. He struggled with some subjects in school, so I gladly gave him the major portion of my help, which seemed to give him greater confidence.

"Welcome to our family," Jack said with a thin smile, on returning home from a business trip shortly after I had moved in. Jack was seldom home by dinner time during the week and was often away on weekends so I saw little of him, but I knew that he and Marion had both signed the necessary papers for me to be transferred to their foster care.

"This is really a miracle, Tom, and you're a very lucky boy!" Sheila, my caseworker, had told me, and then wagging her finger in my face, she added, "This is probably your last chance. Don't mess it up!" I assured her that I had no intention of messing it up.

One night, about five weeks after I had moved in with the Johnsons, I was awakened from sleep by the sound of a door slamming, followed shortly by a loud voice that I recognized at Jack's The voice became louder as Jack moved into a room closer to the bedroom that Jerry and I shared. I glanced over at the other bed and could see in the dim glow of the nightlight that Jerry's eyes were wide open and staring at me.

"Lie still!" he whispered. "If he comes in here, pretend you're sleeping."

Totally confused but sensing the urgency in Jerry's voice and stare, I followed his instructions and closed my eyes as I heard footsteps coming down the hallway, approaching our room. The door opened and someone entered and stood silently between the twin beds. I could hear heavy breathing directly above me and a distinct smell of alcohol drifted toward me, but I kept my eyes closed. After a few minutes that seemed like hours, the bedroom door opened and closed. I opened my eyes and again saw Jerry looking at me with his finger to his lips, cautioning silence.

I listened intently and heard Jack's voice, loud and angry, interrupted with objects crashing to the floor or smashing against a wall.

"God-damn son of a bitch!" Jack screamed. "You don't care how hard I have to work. You don't give a damn. You just spend my money, you freeloading bitch!"

I heard Marion's voice, only faintly, clearly trying to calm him.

"Get your lazy ass out of that bed and make me a sandwich!" he thundered, punctuated by some object hitting the floor.

"Please, Jack," I now heard Marion say, "You'll wake the children."

"The children! The children!" he shouted derisively. "They're probably not even my children, you little whore! Jerry doesn't even look like me, and you bring this new kid into our family because he's probably one of your bastards and you thought you could fool me."

"Jack, you know that's not true. How can you say such a thing?"

"Because you won't sleep with me so you're probably back to your old habits of sleeping with everybody else."

"Jack, I won't sleep with you when you're in this condition and you know I never slept around."

"Bullshit! " A small gap of silence. "I said get out of that bed!" Another crashing sound and then I heard Marion's small, involuntary scream. My heart started racing and the blood was pounding in my ears and every nerve in my body was instantly electrified as that sharp, small scream echoed in my brain, overwhelming me with fear for this person I loved. Then her voice, tremulous and wounded, full of pleading and hurt, rose in desperation.

"Jack, please let go of my hair. Please, Jack, please."

Now their voices rose in volume and I could tell that they were in the hallway leading to all the bedrooms.

"Get into that goddamn kitchen and make me a sandwich, you lazy slut."

"Please stop. You're hurting me."

"I'll break every bone in your goddamn body!"

I heard a thudding noise and another scream. Then I heard Carol's voice, shrill and hysterical.

"Leave my Mommy alone!" she screamed.

Jerry leaped out of his bed and rushed out into the hallway and I was right behind him. I can never forget what I saw, the scene that would burn its image in my brain and haunt me in dreams ever after, evoking all the confusion and fury and pity and fear.

Marion, in a short nightgown, her tangled hair falling in disarray around her face, was crumpled on the floor, leaning against the wall, crying convulsively. Her left hand was rubbing her right shoulder when she had been slammed against the wall. Her body was curled in a protective crouch, her breathing labored amidst her shuddering sobs: I had never seen a person so abjectly defeated, so totally debased. Jack was standing over her, fully dressed, swaying slightly, his eyes glazed, his lips twisted in a smirk.

Carol rushed forward and threw herself down against her mother, cradling Marion's head in her arms and wailing, "Don't cry, Mommy. Don't cry."

Jerry let out a yelp of a wounded animal and charged down the hallway, throwing himself against Jack, his arms flailing wildly. Jack grabbed him roughly under one arm and picked him up off the ground and held him in mid-air, with Jerry kicking and twitching and crying in frustration. Then Jack flicked Jerry away like some discarded cigarette butt and Jerry landed against the opposite wall of the narrow hallway, sliding to the floor, his face a twisted mask of defeat.

Towering over his cringing wife and children, Jack momentarily shifted his attention to me. I had not moved from my bedroom door and was a good ten feet from him.

"You want to get some action too?" he challenged me with a sneer.

I stood frozen to the spot, my head and my heart waging a tumultuous battle. I could do nothing physically to this big, powerful man, except sacrifice myself in defense of those I loved, but if I attempted any futile action against him, I would no doubt lose those I loved and be returned to the Center. My eyes swiveled to Jerry sitting against the opposite wall, his face contorted with outrage, but in that instant when our eyes met, he shook his head slightly from side to side, and I felt that he was instantly assessing the consequences of my intervening and was cautioning me against any action.

Sensing from my moment of hesitation that I would do nothing, Jack barked, "Get the hell back in your room!"

My eyes quickly shifted away from his challenging stare and I meekly obeyed, stepping just inside my bedroom before turning my face to the wall and, fighting back angry tears, reproached myself for my cowardice.

Jack suddenly had had enough.

"The hell with all of you," he said dismissively and then I heard the front door slam again and Carol's voice trying to sooth her mother. I rushed into the hallway and helped Jerry get Marion to her feet.

"I'm sorry, Tom, that you had to see this," she said, her tear-streaked face attempting a small smile as we helped her back to her bedroom. "He's a good man, but whenever he drinks, he's like a possessed person."

Jerry exploded with, "He's a mean bastard and I hate him!"

"Stop that, Jerry! He's your father and he doesn't mean to do these things. Tomorrow it will all be forgotten."

"Mommy, you've got a cut on the side of your head," Carol said, still trying to control her tears.

"And a bruise on your shoulder, too," Jerry said angrily.

"That's when I stumbled and fell against the wall," Marion explained, and we three knew that this was a protective lie but said nothing. "I'll just go to my bathroom and wash up. I'll be out in a minute."

She disappeared behind the closed bathroom door and we stood mutely by her bed, listening to the water running, our emotions still raw from the scene we had just witnessed. Then she came out and offered us a forced smile.

"You should all be back in bed," she said warmly, putting her arms around all of us and herding us toward our bedrooms.

"What if he comes back?" I asked timidly, fear and confusion still tumbling around in my brain.

"He won't be back tonight," Marion said with assurance. "He'll go to his club."

"Mommy, I want to sleep with you," Carol said as we approached the doors of our bedrooms. Marion agreed to this request and kissed us both after Jerry and I had returned to our beds. Bending over me she said, "Tom, I'm really sorry. I thought that maybe with you as a new member of our family, Jack might be different." There was a long pause as tears appeared again at the corners of her eyes. "Please don't think badly of him. It's just the drink...he can't help himself."

I reached up and hugged her. "I don't want you to be hurt!" I cried.

"I know. I know," she said, returning my hug. "I'll be fine. Now go to sleep."

She turned off the light and closed the door and I lay in the darkened stillness, wide awake, trying to come to terms with everything that had just happened, feeling guilty and helpless. Out of the darkness I heard Jerry's voice.

"There's nothing you could have done," he reassured me, as if reading my thoughts. "It's better if you stay out of it."

"Does this happen a lot?" I asked.

"Only when he gets really drunk. Then he's a mean drunk," Jerry said with disgust.

"Does he always hit her?"

"Sometimes he just screams and throws things but you can never tell what he might do. Once he came in here when I was sleeping and yanked me out of bed and made me shine his shoes. He said I should start earning my keep, whatever that means."

I was weighing this new information when Jerry said, "He's got a girlfriend. He even showed me her picture when he was drunk one time, and he told me that she knew how to take care of him, unlike Mon, he said, who neglected him."

"Does your Mom know?"

"Sure. He throws her up to Mom a lot when he's drunk."

"Why doesn't she leave him?"

"She can't. He's got all the money and she's got no place to go, no family except us and she'd never leave us."

"She doesn't have any relatives?" I asked.

"No, she was an orphan. She never knew her mother or father."

This startling piece of news made me love her more and it also made me realize why she seemed to have such empathy for my situation.

"Besides," Jerry added, with a clear note of confusion in his voice, "she says she still loves him and wants us all to be a family."

"I'm sorry," was all I could think of to say.

"Yeah," said Jerry. "Me too."

Then, from emotional exhaustion, I fell asleep, only to awaken several times during the remainder of the night from bad dreams.

* * * *

The next morning Marion greeted us in the kitchen with her usual cheerfulness and no one made any mention of the horrors of the night. She wore a head scarf to cover the cut on her forehead and her dress covered the bruises on her shoulder and upper arm. Taking a cue from Marion, Carol and Jerry acted as if nothing unusual had occurred, no doubt wanting to soothe their mother. I found the morning's "let's pretend nothing happened" rituals to be almost as scary as the previous violence and wanted to shout and holler and punch something, anything, and tell her how much I loved her and wanted to protect her, vowing that I'd never let him touch her again and fantasizing about some way we could kill him if he ever did this again. Instead I played along with the charade, quietly ate my breakfast and kissed her goodbye before going off to school.

There were other nights of violent scenes and screaming children, usually heralded by the front door slamming--an instant alarm that electrified my body and put all my brain waves on alert, waiting to see what havoc Jack might have in store for us at this drunken, deranged performance. While he shoved and pushed Jerry whenever Jerry went to his mother's defense, he reserved the slapping and punching and dragging and brutal denunciations for Marion. The next day all the hurt, both physical and psychological, would be masked with an air of normality. No one ever knew what took place in Penthouse B, outside of us five, except probably the people below us. When Sheila, my caseworker, visited, we presented a united front of the perfect family.

"I wish all my foster families were as wonderful as yours, Mrs. Johnson," Sheila would say before departing. "Tom's a very lucky boy!" She'd smile at me, but her eyes had that stern, "don't mess up" look, and I'd look away.

Inwardly I was disintegrating. On Jerry's strong urging and even a few offhand remarks from Marion, I remained a bystander at these horrific confrontations, which cost me great emotional turmoil.

"It's funny now, Tom," Jerry remarked to me, "but Mom and I thought he might not be so mean if another person was present all the time, but that hasn't bothered him at all."

Eventually, though, it did bother him, for I could not play a role as good as Jerry or even Carol and my sullenness and hostile stares when in his presence clearly annoyed him. Finally, after ten months, he demanded that I be returned to the children's center. Marion and Jerry and Carol fought as hard as they could for me, but, of course, he prevailed. He had a lengthy conference with Sheila, the details of which I never learned, but from all her subsequent interactions with me, she clearly considered me an incorrigibly bad boy.

The day of my departure from the Johnson home lives indelibly in my memory for, once again, I was losing my family. Jerry insisted that I take a dozen of his most treasured baseball cards, and Carol had written me a poem that she pressed into my hand as we stood in the foyer of their apartment, waiting for the elevator. Marion, misty-eyed, kept smoothing my hair and repeating "I'm so sorry, Tom." There were tears and long hugs and promises that we would remain a family forever but that was not to be.

For about six months after my return to the center, Marion continued her volunteer work and I saw her twice a week. She'd bring me books with little notes hidden inside, from both Jerry and Carol, telling me how much they all missed me and what they were up to. Several times I could see the thick layer of make-up covering facial bruises and then one day, without any warning or explanation or farewell, she wasn't there and I never saw her again. In my locker next to my cot I now kept three pictures: one of my parents and me, all dressed up and smiling on the day that I had made my First Communion; the one of me on my fourteenth birthday; and one of Marion, Jerry, Carol and me, taken in Central Park when we were all momentarily forgetful and happy. We're standing in a row with arms around one another in front of the Children's Zoo that Carol loved so much.

Despite all the underlying tumult and debasement in the Johnson household, it's the smiling interlocked people in that picture whom I remember and cherish for offering me refuge and a renewed sense of self-worth. Still, as my recurrent dream indicates, I'm haunted by the beautiful, smiling woman in the picture, for what I could not do for her.

* * * *

I lived with one other foster family briefly, sometime after being with the Johnsons, but that was a disaster. One day when I was sixteen, I ran away from the Queens apartment where this family lived and traveled to the Johnsons' apartment on Manhattan's Central Park West. The doorman and I recognized each other and he told me that the Johnsons had moved out of state—he didn't know where—over a year ago. That ended my dream of a loving reunion.

I joined the Army at seventeen and by the time I was discharged on my twenty-first birthday, I had become a man, determined to put all the sorrows and disappointments of childhood behind me. I returned to New York City, enrolled in City University and took a night job as a bartender. One day during the spring semester of my junior year, while having lunch in a campus cafeteria, I was approached by a girl who looked vaguely familiar.

"Are you Tom Littleton?" the girl asked.

"Yes," I replied, staring at the girl holding a lunch tray, trying to place her.

"I thought it was you, though I wasn't sure. You've changed quite a bit since you were fourteen. But then I guess I've changed a lot since I was nine."

"Carol!" I shouted, truly happy to see her.

"Yes," she affirmed with a wide grin and I swept her into my arms.

"What are you doing here?" I asked.

""I'm a freshman," she responded good-naturedly.

I did some quick mental math.

"My god, that's right! I'm twenty-four so you must be nineteen." Carol nodded affirmatively. "Let's find some table in the cafeteria annex where it's usually less crowded and we can talk," I suggested.

We found an empty table and, disregarding our lunches, focused on catching up. She insisted that I go first and in a few short sentences I covered my Army and college years. "I tried to track you down, but you had moved out of state. I even came to your apartment building a year or so after I left you. Now that's all for me," I said. "Tell me about you and Jerry and your mother."

Carol's smile disappeared and her eyelids lowered. Her gaze shifted from me to the table.

"My mother's dead, Tom. She died four years ago."

"Oh, god, no!" I shouted, drawing stares from nearly tables. As though reeling from a body blow, I crouched over the table. My guts were churning and my brain was struggling to comprehend this startling, devastating news. I felt as confused and overwhelmed as I did when the police came to my school with a neighbor to tell me of my parents' death by the runaway bus.

"What happened?" I struggled to ask.

"A brain hemorrhage," Carol said. "She was at home, after dinner. Jerry and I were there. We were all watching television and Mom said she had a splitting headache and felt dizzy and she went to her room to lie down. I went in about an hour later to see how she was and she was unconscious. Jerry called 911 and she was rushed to the hospital, but they couldn't save her and she died the next morning."

Tears were visible at the corners of her eyes, as they were in mine.

"Oh, Carol, I'm so sorry," was all I could muster because I was struggling with my own sense of loss, but seeing how hard she was trying to keep her composure, I rallied on. "How awful for you and Jerry! How is he?"

Now her words came more slowly and tears streaked her cheeks.

"Jerry's a mess, I'm afraid," she said, still gazing downward at the table and speaking in a monotone voice. "He got heavily into drugs as a teenager, went through several rehabilitation programs but nothing stuck. Then when Mom died, he went crazy, got hooked again and one day he just disappeared and no one's heard from him now for over three years."

Carol's voice sunk to almost a whisper with this last sentence. I thought of Jerry as the sweet, generous, loving kid who had become like a brother to me and who had ambitious dreams, and I ached to think of him aimlessly wandering the country, broken and defeated, living only for his next fix. Sorrow and pity for these loved ones were tearing at me, to be replaced by hard, cold fury.

"What about Jack?" I asked through clenched teeth.

"Shortly after you left us," Carol said, "he sobered up for a short time and things were okay—we were even thinking he might agree to bringing you back to live with us. Mom talked about you all the time. But then he fell off the wagon and things really got bad and he was abusing her regularly."

"That must have been when she was still coming to the refuge center and I saw the heavy makeup covering her bruises," I said, thinking aloud, and Carol nodded yes before continuing.

"He left his law firm and accepted a position with the federal government and insisted that we move to Washington D.C."

"She never said goodbye," I interjected, carried back to my confusion and despair when she disappeared from my life.

Carol nodded. "Jerry and I wanted to go see you before we left New York, but Mom just couldn't bear the thought of another tearful goodbye." She paused. "I guess it was cowardly, Tom, but she was under so much strain."

I nodded and Carol continued. "Mom thought this might be a new start but it was just the same old shit! When she passed away I was fourteen, and he brought me back to live with his mother, my grandma, in New Rochelle. Jerry had just turned eighteen and was away at college before dropping out for good and then disappearing. My father stayed in Washington and I hardly ever see him."

Carol paused as if weighing her words.

"There's a reason he doesn't want to see me, Tom," she said, and her voice took on a darker tone than I had ever heard. She looked directly into my eyes.

"He killed her! He killed her and he knows I know he killed her!"

The old feelings of fear and horror raced across my nervous system and I could say nothing. Carol continued.

"She had finally decided to leave him. She went public and filed for a separation and after he had moved out of the house, thinking that with just a short separation she'd take him back, she got an order of protection against him and he went ballistic. One night in a drunken rage, he broke in through the back door of our house and attacked her. I saw it all. She ran to the phone to call the police but he yanked the cord out of the wall and then…"

Carol's voice rose in pitch and her eyes were glazed as she relived what she described next. "…then he grabbed her by her hair as she tried to run away from him and he smashed her hard across her face and her head hit the wall and he yanked her back by her hair and hit her again and again, holding her firmly in place by her hair. 'You think you can keep me out of my own house, bitch?' he kept shouting over and over.

"I was screaming for him to stop and I jumped on his back and was hitting him on the back of his head with my fists, but he didn't stop. Only when I bit him on his neck did he finally let go of her hair and she crumpled to the floor. Then he turned to me. 'You're just like your mother,' he said with a sneer and raised his hand to hit me, but I eluded him and ran out the front door and went to our neighbors' house and asked them to call the police. Than I ran back to our house and he was gone and my mother was gone too. I found her in the bathroom applying cold water to her face.

"When the police came, I told them what my father had done but my mother, whose face was swollen, refused to press charges and never mentioned that she had an order of protection against him. I couldn't convince her to go to the hospital emergency room or to see her doctor. In a few days the swelling went down but then she started complaining of headaches."

I suddenly exploded with "Why the hell didn't she press charges against the bastard?" White-hot rage was sweeping over me.

"I don't know," Carol said abstractly. "I guess at some level she still loved him and maybe she kept hoping that if he could only break his bondage to booze, the wonderful man she married might return. Who knows? Anyway, in two weeks she was dead. And no one can tell me that those blows to her head didn't bring on an internal hemorrhage."

"Didn't anyone ever make the connection?" I asked, incensed with the injustice of it all.

Carol responded quickly. "No. I was afraid what Jerry might do if I said anything: he'd want to kill his father, so I said nothing since I didn't want to lose him, too. He never knew." Then she paused and looked off into the distance. "Of course, the irony is that I lost him anyway," she said softly, her lower lip trembling. "You're the only person I've ever told the whole story to, Tom."

I tried to console her as best I could while still stunned and angered by all these reported events. We met frequently during my senior year and talked a lot about our good memories. I think it helped both of us. We never lost contact after that and I still consider her my little sister.

* * * *

The sun has now swept across the entire room and I'm surprised to see, when I glance at my watch, that I've been lost in memories for nearly an hour. Now it's almost as if the sun is flooding my brain for suddenly, in a lightning streak of perfect clarity, I realize what the missing piece of the puzzle is, and why Dr. Roth told me I had to find it for myself.

Despite my vivid recall of the violent eruptions I witnessed and the inner turmoil I experienced, I had never really come to terms with my cautious responses, choosing self-protection over loyalty. I never tried to help Marion, telling myself it was fruitless, but that's just the point. Love is not a rational force; it's fiercely illogical, irreducible to points A, B and C.

Recriminations were filling my head. I should have stood up for Marion instead of protecting my own precarious position in the family. My own future might have been jeopardized but I might have saved her; I should have spoken up instead of joining the conspiracy of silence and pretending to the world that nothing was amiss. I should have shown Marion how much I loved her, despite the consequences. Maybe that would have given her the extra push she needed to free herself earlier from her husband's tyranny. I should have confronted Jack the way Jerry did, demonstrating that although he could physically hurt me and cast me out of his family, I would still defend inviolate rules of right and wrong, as taught me by my parents, for the person I loved.

The sun is blinding my eyes but I don't move, still lost in reflection. I've always been guarded and cautious. Yes, I can use the excuse of my parents' sudden death and the ensuing dislocation that forged my alienation and filled me with self-pity and rage and caused me to erect an emotional wall around me. But when Marion came into my life and, also being an orphan, brought empathy and loving validation and I, in turn, loved her wholeheartedly, I still held back and placed conditions on my love when faced with challenges to it.

Then it occurs to me that somehow my wife has sensed this for a long time. We go along, each in our own way, focusing mostly on our kids and our immediate goals. But she knows! She knows! She knows that my love will always be conditional; will always be based on a rational weighing and assessing; will always be forthcoming only after evaluating all the pro's and con's of our relationship and finding a positive balance; will always place a self-protective shield against the uncertainty of total, unconditional commitment.

A vivid image of Marion I now see before me and her sweet, smiling face transmutes into my wife's. Then I know something with certainty. Marion loved me unconditionally, just as my wife, at the outset of our courtship and marriage, loved me unreservedly, before sensing the limitations I set on my reciprocity.

Dr. Roth had said that all children who suddenly lose their parents feel abandoned and their anger is mixed with self-pity and a new defense mechanism of blunted emotions driven by caution, in an effort to reduce any further exposure to hurt. Then I think of my mother, so central to my emotional well-being for the twelve years I had her, and so generous in her uninhibited affection and demonstrations of love. In my anger at losing her, I repudiated her example and had played my emotionally guarded game ever since.

These three wonderful women—my wife, my mother and my foster mother—were showing me the way to redemption. Now I just had to follow.

Purely on impulse, I pick up the phone and dial my wife's work number, knowing my unexpected call with no specific purpose or urgent message will surprise and, I hope, delight her. It's a first small gesture.